Contents

By Rock and Pool on an Austral Shore, and Other Stories

Louis Becke

BY ROCK AND POOL
ON AN AUSTRAL SHORE,
AND OTHER STORIES

BY

Louis Becke

By Rock and Pool on an Austral Shore

The quaint, old-fashioned little town faces eastward to the blue Pacific, whose billows, when the wind blows from any point between north and east, come tumbling in across the shallow bar in ceaseless lines of foaming white, to meet, when the tide is on the ebb, the swift current of a tidal river as broad as the Thames at Westminster Bridge. On the south side of the bar, from the sleepy town itself to the pilot station on the Signal Hill, there rises a series of smooth grassy bluffs, whose seaward bases touch the fringe of many small beaches, or start sheer upward from the water when the tide is high, and the noisy swish and swirl of the eager river current has ceased.

As you stand on the Signal Hill, and look along the coast, you see a long, long monotonous line of beach, trending northward ten miles from end to end, forming a great curve from the sandspit on the north side of the treacherous bar to the blue loom of a headland in shape like the figure of a couchant lion. Back from the shore-line, a narrow littoral of dense scrub, impervious to the rays of the sun, and unbroken in its solitude except by the cries of birds, or the heavy footfall of wild cattle upon the thick carpet of fallen leaves; and then, far to the west, the dimmed, shadowy outline of the main coastal range.

*   *   *   *   *

It is a keen, frosty morning in June--the midwinter of Australia--and as the red sun bursts through the sea-rim, a gentle land breeze creeps softly down from the mountain forest of gums and iron-barks, and blows away the mists that, all through a night of cloudless calm, have laid heavily upon the surface of the sleeping ocean. One by one the doors of the five little white-painted, weather-boarded houses which form the quarters of the pilot-boat's crew open, and five brown, hairy-faced men, each smoking a pipe, issue forth, and, hands in pockets, scan the surface of the sea from north to south, for perchance a schooner, trying to make the port, may have been carried along by the current from the southward, and is within signalling distance to tell her whether the bar is passable or not. For the bar of the Port is as changeable in its moods as the heart of a giddy maid to her lovers--to-day it may invite you to come in and take possession of its placid waters in the harbour beyond; to-morrow it may roar and snarl with boiling surf and savage, eddying currents, and whirlpools slapping fiercely against the grim, black rocks of the southern shore.

Look at the five men as they stand or saunter about on the smooth, frosty grass. They are sailormen--one and all--as you can see by their walk and hear by their talk; rough, ready, and sturdy, though not so sturdy nor so square-built as your solid men of brave old Deal; but a long way better in appearance and character than the sponging, tip-seeking, loafing fraternity of slouching, lazy robbers who on the parades of Brighton, Hastings, and Eastbourne, and other fashionable seaside resorts in this country, lean against lamp-posts with "Licensed Boatman" writ on their hat-bands, and call themselves fishermen, though they seldom handle a herring or cod that does not come from a fishmonger's shop. These Australians of British blood are leaner in face, leaner in limb than the Kentish men, and drink whiskey instead of coffee or tea at early morn. But see them at work in the face of danger and death on that bar, when the surf is leaping high and a schooner lies broadside on and helpless to the sweeping rollers, and you will say that a more undaunted crew never gripped an oar to rescue a fellow-sailorman from the hungry sea.

One of them, a grey-haired, deeply-bronzed man of sixty, with his neck and hands tatooed in strange markings, imprinted thereon by the hands of the wild natives of Tucopia, in the South Seas, with whom he has lived forty years before as one of themselves, is mine own particular friend and crony, for his two sons have been playmates with my brothers and myself, who were all born in this quaint old-time seaport of the first colony in Australia; this forgotten remnant of the dread days of the awful convict system, when the clank of horrible gyves sounded on the now deserted and grass-grown streets, and the swish of the hateful and ever active "cat" was heard within the walls of the huge red-brick prison on the bluff facing the sea. Oh, the old, old memories of those hideous times! How little they wounded or troubled our boyish minds, as we, bent on some fishing or hunting venture along the coast, walked along a road which had been first soddened by tears and then dried by the panting, anguished breathings of beings fashioned in the image of their Creator, as they toiled and died under the brutal hands of their savage taskmasters--the civilian officials of that cruel "System" which, by the irony of fate, the far-seeing, gentle, and tender-hearted Arthur Phillip, the founder of Australia, was first appointed to administer.

But away with such memories for the moment. Over the lee side with them into the Sea of the Past, together with the clank of the fetters and the hum of the cat and the merciless laws of the time; sink them all together with the names of the military rum-selling traducers of the good Phillip, and of ill-tempered, passionate sailor Bligh of the ***Bounty***--honest, brave, irascible, vindictive; destroyer of his ship's company on that fateful adventure to Tahiti, hero of the most famous boat-voyage the world has ever known; sea-bully and petty "hazer" of hapless Fletcher Christian and his comrades, gallant officer in battle and thanked by Nelson at Copenhagen; conscientious governor of a starveling colony gasping under the hands of unscrupulous military money-makers, William Bligh deserves to be remembered by all men of English blood who are proud of the annals of the most glorious navy in the world.

*   *   *   *   *

But ere we descend to the beach to wander by rock and pool in this glowing Australian sun, the warm, loving rays of which are fast drying the frost-coated grass, let us look at these square, old-time monuments to the dead, placed on the Barrack Hill, and overlooking the sea. There are four in all, but around them are many low, sunken headstones of lichen-covered slabs, the inscriptions on which, like many of those on the stones in the cemetery by the reedy creek, have long since vanished.

There, indeed, if you care to brave the snake-haunted place you will discover a word, or the part of a word--"Talav----," "Torre----Vedras," "Vimiera," or "Badaj----," or "Fuentes de On----," and you know that underneath lies the dust of men who served their country well when the Iron Duke was rescuing Europe from the grip of the bloodstained Corsican. On one, which for seventy years has faced the rising sun and the salty breath of the ocean breeze, there remains but the one glorious word, "Aboukir!" every indented letter thickly filled with grey moss and lichen, though the name of he who fought there has disappeared, and being but that of some humble seaman, is unrecorded and unknown in the annals of his country. How strange it seems! but yet how fitting that this one word alone should be preserved by loving Nature from the decaying touch of Time. Perhaps the very hand of the convict mason who held the chisel to the stone struck deeper as he carved the letters of the name of the glorious victory.

But let us away from here; for in the hot summer months amid these neglected and decaying memorials of the dead, creeping and crawling in and out of the crumbling masonry of the tombs, gliding among the long, reedy grass, or lying basking in the sun upon the fallen headstones, are deadly black and brown snakes. They have made this old, time-forgotten cemetery their own favourite haunting place; for the waters of the creek are near, and on its margin they find their prey. Once, so the shaky old wharfinger will tell you, a naval lieutenant, who had been badly wounded in the first Maori war, died in the commandant's house. He was buried here on the bank of the creek, and one day his young wife who had come from England to nurse him and found him dead, sat down on his grave and went to sleep. When she awoke, a great black snake was lying on her knees. She died that day from the shock.

The largest of these four monuments on the bluff stands nearest to the sea, and the inscription on the heavy flat slab of sandstone which covers it is fairly legible:--

Sacred to the Memory of
JAMES VAUGHAN,
Who was a Private in Captain
Fraser Allan's Company
of the 40th Regiment, Who died on the 24th November, 1823,
of a Gunshot Wound Received
on the 20th Day of the Month,
when in Pursuit of a

Runaway Convict.

Aged 25 years.

The others record the names of the "infant son and daughters of Mr. G. Smith, Commissariat Storekeeper," and of "Edward Marvin, who died 4th July, 1821, aged 21 years."

Many other sunken headstones denote the last resting-places of soldiers and sailors, and civilian officials, who died between 1821 and 1830, when the little port was a thriving place, and when, as the old gossips will tell you, it made a "rare show, when the Governor came here, and Major Innes--him as brought that cussed lantana plant from the Peninsula--sent ninety mounted men to escort him to Lake Innes."

*   *   *   *   *

The tide is low, and the flat *congewoi*-covered ledges of reef on the southern side of the bar lie bare and exposed to the sun. Here and there in the crystal pools among the rocks, fish have been left by the tide, and as you step over the *congewoi*, whose teats spurt out jets of water to the pressure of your foot, large silvery bream and gaily-hued parrot-fish rush off and hide themselves from view. But tear off a piece of *congewoi*, open it, and throw the sanguinary-coloured delicacy into the water, and presently you will see the parrot-fish dart out eagerly, and begin to tear it asunder with their long, irregular, and needle-like teeth, whilst the more cautious and lordly bream, with wary eye and gentle, undulating tail, watch from underneath a ledge for a favourable moment to dash out and secure a morsel.

In some of the wider and shallower ponds are countless thousands of small mullet, each about three or four inches in length, and swimming closely together in separated but compact battalions. Some, as the sound of a human footstep warns them of danger, rush for safety among the submerged clefts and crevices of their temporary retreat, only to be mercilessly and fatally enveloped by the snaky, viscous tentacles of the ever-lurking octopus, for every hole and pool among the rocks contains one or more of these hideously repulsive creatures.

Sometimes you will see one crawling over the *congewoi*, changing from one pool to another in search of prey; its greeny-grey eyes regard you with defiant malevolence. Strike it heavily with a stick, or thrust it through with a spear, and in an instant its colour, which a moment before was either a dark mottled brown or a mingled reddish-black, changes to a ghastly, horrible, marbled grey; the horrid tentacles writhe and cling to the weapon, or spread out and adhere to the surrounding points of rock, a black, inky fluid is ejected from the soft, pulpy, and slimy body; and then, after raining blow after blow upon it, it lies unable to crawl away, but still twisting and turning, and showing its red and white suckers--a thing of horror indeed, the embodiment of all that is hateful, wicked, and malignant in nature.

Some idea of the numbers of these crafty and savage denizens of the limpid pools may be obtained by dropping a baited fishing line in one of the deeper spots. First you will see one, and then another, thin end of a tentacle come waveringly out from underneath a ledge of rock, and point towards the bait, then the rest of the ugly creature follows, and gathering itself together, darts upon the hook, for the possession of which half a dozen more of its fellows are already advancing, either swimming or by drawing themselves over the sandy bottom of the pool. Deep buried in the sand itself is another, a brute which may weigh ten or fifteen pounds, and which would take all the strength of a strong man to overcome were its loathsome tentacles clasped round his limbs in their horrid embrace. Only part of the head and the half-closed, tigerish eyes are visible, and even these portions are coated over with fine sand so as to render them almost undistinguishable from the bed in which it lies awaiting for some careless crab or fish to come within striking distance. How us boys delighted to destroy these big fellows when we came across one thus hidden in the sand or *debris* on the bottom! A quick thrust of the spear through the tough, elongated head, a vision of whirling, outspread, red and black snaky tentacles, and then the thing is dragged out by main strength and dashed down upon the rocks, to be struck with waddies or stones until the spear can be withdrawn. Everything, it is said, has its use in this world, and the octopus is eminently useful to the Australian line fisherman, for the bream, trevally, flathead, jew-fish, and the noble schnapper dearly love its tough, white flesh, especially after the creature has been held over a flame for a few minutes, so that the mottled skin may be peeled off.

But treacherous and murderous Thug of the Sea as he is, the octopus has one dreaded foe before whom he flees in terror, and compresses his body into the narrowest and most inaccessible cleft or endeavours to bury himself in the loose, soft sand--and that foe is the orange-coloured or sage-green rock eel. Never do you see one of these eels in the open water; they lie deep under the stones or twine their lithe, slippery bodies among the waving kelp or seaweed. Always hungry, savage-eyed, and vicious, they know no fear of any living thing, and seizing an octopus and biting off tentacle after tentacle with their closely-set, needle-like teeth and swallowing it whole is a matter of no more moment to them than the bolting of a tender young mullet or bream. In vain does the Sea Thug endeavour to enwrap himself round and round the body of one of these sinuous, scaleless sea-snakes and fasten on to it with his terrible cupping apparatus of suckers--the eel slips in and out and "wolfs" and worries his enemy without the slightest harm to itself. Some of them are large--especially the orange-coloured variety--three or four feet in length, and often one will raise his snaky head apparently out of solid rock and regard you steadily for a moment. Then he disappears. You advance cautiously to the spot and find a hole no larger than the circumference of an afternoon tea cup, communicating with the water beneath. Lower a baited hook with a strong wire snooding, and "Yellowskin" will open wide his jaws and swallow it without your feeling the slightest movement of the line. But you must be quick and strong of hand then, or you will never drag him forth, for slippery as he is he can coil his length around a projecting bit of rock and defy you for perhaps five or ten minutes; and then when you do succeed in tearing him away and pull him out with the hook buried deep in his loose, pendulous, wrinkled and corduroyed throat, he instantly resolves himself into a quivering Gordian knot, winding the line in and about his coils and knotting it into such knots that can never be unravelled.

Here and there you will see lying buried deep in the growing coral, or covered with black masses of *congewoi* such things as iron and copper bolts, or heavy pieces of squared timber, the relics of the many wrecks that have occurred on the bar--some recent, some in years long gone by. Out there, lying wedged in between the weed and kelp-covered boulders, only visible at low water, are two of the guns of the ill-fated *Wanderer*, a ship, like her owner, famous in the history of the colony. She was the property of a Mr. Benjamin Boyd, a man of flocks and herds and wealth, who founded a town and a great whaling station on the shores of Twofold Bay, where he employed some hundreds of men, bond and free. He was of an adventur-ous and restless disposition, and after making several voyages to the South Seas, was cruelly cut off and murdered by the cannibal natives of Guadalcanar in the Solomon Islands, in the "fifties." The captain, after beating off the savages, who, having killed poor Boyd on shore, made a determined attempt to capture the ship, set sail for Aus-tralia, and in endeavouring to cross in over the bar went ashore and became a total wreck. Here is a description written by Judge McFarland of the **Wanderer** as she was in those days when Boyd dreamed a dream of founding a Republic in the South Sea Islands with his wild crew of Polynesians and a few white fellow adventurers:--

"She was of 240 tons burthen; very fleet, and had a flush deck; and her cabins were fitted up with every possible attention to convenience, and with great ele-gance; and had she been intended as a war craft, she could scarcely have been more powerfully armed, for she carried four brass deck-guns--two six-pounders and two four-pounders--mounted on carriages resembling dolphins, four two-pounder rail guns--two on each side--and one brass twelve-pounder traversing gun (which had seen service at Waterloo)--in all thirteen serviceable guns. Besides these, there were two small, highly-ornamented guns used for firing signals, which were said to have been obtained from the wreck of the **Royal George** at Spithead. There were also provided ample stores of round shot and grape for the guns, and a due proportion of small arms, boarding pikes, tomahawks, &c."

Half a mile further on, and we are under the Signal Hill, and standing on one side of a wide, flat rock, through which a boat passage has been cut by convict hands, when first the white tents of the soldiers were seen on the Barrack Hill. And here, at this same spot, more than a hundred years ago, and thirty before the sound of the axe was first heard amid the forest or tallow-woods and red gum, there once landed a strange party of sea-worn, haggard-faced beings--six men, one woman, and two infant children. They were the unfortunate Bryant party--whose won-derful and daring voyage from Sydney to Timor in a wretched, ill-equipped boat, ranks second only to that of Bligh himself. For Will Bryant, an ex-smuggler who was leader, had heard of Bligh's voyage in the boat belonging to the **Bounty**; and fired with the desire to escape with his wife and children from the famine-stricken community on the shores of Port Jackson, he and his companions in servitude stole a small fishing-boat and boldly put to sea to face a journey of more that three thousand miles over an unknown and dangerous ocean. A few weeks after leaving Sydney they had sighted this little nook when seeking refuge from a fierce north-easterly gale, and here they remained for many days, so that the woman and children might gain strength and the seams of the leaking boat be payed with tallow--their only substitute for oakum. Then onward they sailed or rowed, for long, long weary weeks, landing here and there on the coast to seek for water and shell-fish, harried and chased by cannibal savages, suffering all the agonies that could be suffered on such a wild venture, until they reached Timor, only by a strange and unhappy fate to fall into the hands of the brutal and infamous Edwards of the ***Pandora*** frigate, who with his wrecked ship's company, and the surviving and manacled mutineers of the ***Bounty***, who had surrendered to him, soon afterwards appeared at the Dutch port. Bryant, the daring leader, was so fortunate as to die of fever, and so escaped the fate in store for his comrades. 'Tis a strange story indeed.

*   *   *   *   *

At the end of the point of brown, rugged rocks which form a natural breakwater to this tiny boat harbour, the water is deep, showing a pale transparent green at their base, and deep inpenetrable blue ten fathoms beyond. To-day, because it is mid-winter, and the wind blows from the west, the sea is clearer than ever, and far down below will be discerned lazily swimming to and fro great reddish-brown or bright blue groper, watching the dripping sides of the rock in hope that some of the active, gaily-hued crabs which scurry downwards as you approach may fall in--for the blue groper is a ***gourmet***, disdaining to eat of his own tribe, and caring only for crabs or the larger and more luscious crayfish. Stand here when the tide is high and the surf is sweeping in creamy sheets over the lower ledges of rocks; and as the water pours off torrent-like from the surface and leaves them bare, you may oft behold a huge fish--aye, or two or three--lying kicking on its side with a young crayfish in its thick, fleshy jaws, calmly waiting for the next sea to set him afloat again. Brave fellows are these gropers--forty, fifty, up to seventy pounds sometimes, and dangerous fish to hook in such a place as this, where a false step may send a man headlong into the surf below with his line tangled round his feet or arms. But on such a morning as this one might fall overboard and come to no harm, for the sea is smooth, and the kelp sways but gently to the soft rise and fall of the water, and seldom in these cold days of June does Jack Shark cruise in under the lee of the rocks. It is in November, hot, sweltering November, when the clinking sand of the shining beach is burning to the booted foot, and the countless myriads of terrified sea salmon come swarming in over the bar on their way to spawn in the river beyond, that he and his fellows and the bony-snouted saw-fish rush to and fro in the shallow waters, driving their prey before them, and gorging as they drive, till the clear waters of the bar are turned into a bloodied froth. At such a time as this it might be bad to fall overboard, though some of the local youths give but little more heed to the tigers of the sea than they do to the accompanying drove of harmless porpoises, which join in the onslaught on the hapless salmon.

A mile eastward from the shore there rises stark and clear a great dome-shaped rock, the haunt and resting-place of thousands of snow-white gulls and brown-plumaged boobies. The breeding-place of the former is within rifle-shot--over there on that long stretch of banked-up sand on the north side of the bar, where, amid the shelter of the coarse, tufted grass the delicate, graceful creatures will sit three months hence on their fragile white and purple-splashed eggs. The boobies are but visitors, for their breeding-places are on the bleak, savage islands far to the south, amid the snows and storms of black Antarctic seas. But here they dwell together, in unison with the gulls, and were the wind not westerly you could hear their shrill cries and hoarse croaking as they wheel and eddy and circle above the lonely rock, on the highest pinnacle of which a great fish-eagle, with neck thrown back upon his shoulders and eyes fixed eastward to the sun, stands oblivious of their clamour, as creatures beneath his notice.

Once round the southern side of the Signal Hill the noise of the bar is lost. Between the hill and the next point--a wild, stern-looking precipice of black-trap rock--there lies a half a mile or more of shingly strand, just such as you would see at Pevensey Bay or Deal, but backed up at high-water mark with piles of drift timber--great dead trees that have floated from the far northern rivers, their mighty branches and netted roots bleached white by the sun and wind of many years, and smelling sweet of the salty sea air. Mingled with the lighter bits of driftwood and heaps of seaweed are the shells of hundreds of crayfish--some of the largest are newly cast up by the sea, and the carapace is yellow and blue; others are burnt red by exposure to the sun; while almost at every step you crush into the thin backs and armoured tails of young ones about a foot in length, the flesh of which, by some mysterious process of nature, has vanished, leaving the skin, muscles, and beautiful fan-like tail just as fresh as if the crustaceans were alive. Just here, out among those kelp-covered rocks, you may, on a moonlight night, catch as many crayfish as you wish--three of them will be as much as any one would care to carry a mile, for a large, full-grown "lobster," as they are called locally, will weigh a good ten pounds.

Once round the precipice we come to a new phase of coastal scenery. From the high land above us green scrub-covered spur after spur shoots downward to the shore, enclosing numerous little beaches of coarse sand and many coloured spiral shells--"Reddies" we boys called them--with here and there a rare and beautiful cowrie of banded jet black and pearly white. The sea-wall of rock has here but few pools, being split up into long, deep, and narrow chasms, into which the gentle ocean swell comes with strange gurglings and hissings, and groan-like sounds, and tiny jets of spray spout up from hundreds of air-holes through the hollow crust of rock. Here for the first time since the town was left, are heard the cries of land birds; for in the wild apple and rugged honeysuckle trees which grow on the rich, red soil of the spurs they are there in plenty--crocketts, king parrots, leatherheads, "butcher" and "bell" birds, and the beautiful bronze-wing pigeon--while deep within the silent gullies you constantly hear the little black scrub wallabies leaping through the undergrowth and fallen leaves, to hide in still darker forest recesses above.

There are snakes here, too. Everywhere their sinuous tracks are visible on the sand, criss-crossing with the more defined scratchy markings of those of iguanas. The latter we know come down to carry off any dead fish cast ashore by the waves, or to seize any live ones which may be imprisoned in a shallow pool; but what brings the deadly brown and black snakes down to the edge of *salt* water at night time?

Point after point, tiny bay after bay, and then we come to a wider expanse of clear, stoneless beach, at the farther end of which a huge boulder of jagged, yellow rock, covered on the summit with a thick mantle of a pale green, fleshly-leaved creeper, bearing a pink flower. It stands in a deep pool about a hundred yards in circumference, and as like as not we shall find the surface of the water covered by thousands of green-backed, red-billed garfish and silvery mullet, whose very numbers prevent them from escaping. Scores of them leap out upon the sand, and lie there with panting gill and flapping tail. It is a great place for us boys, for here at low tides in the winter we strip off, and with naked hands catch the mullet and gars and silvery-sided trumpeters, and throw them out on the beach, to be grilled later on over a fire of glowing honeysuckle cobs, and eaten without salt. What boy does care about such a thing as salt at such times, when his eye is bright and his skin glows with the flush of health, and the soft murmuring of the sea is mingling in his ears with the thrilling call of the birds, and the rustling hum of the bush; and the yellow sun shines down from a glorious sky of cloudless blue, and dries the sand upon his naked feet; and the very joy of being alive, and away from school, is happiness enough in itself!

For here, by rock and pool on this lonely Austral beach, it is good and sweet for man or boy to be, and, if but in utter idleness, to watch and listen--and think.

Solepa

The last strokes of the bell for evening service had scarce died away when I heard a footstep on the pebbly path, and old Pakia, staff in hand and pipe dangling from his pendulous ear-lobe, walked quietly up the steps and sat down cross-legged on the verandah. All my own people had gone to church and the house was very quiet.

"Good evening, Pakia," I said in English, "how are you, old man?"

A smile lit up the brown, old, wrinkled face as he heard my voice--for I was lying down in the sitting-room, smoking my after-supper pipe--as he answered in the island dialect that he was well, but that his house was in darkness and he, being lonely, had come over to sit with me awhile.

"That is well, Pakia, for I too am lonely, and who so good as thee to talk with when the mind is heavy and the days are long, and no sail cometh up from the sea-rim? Come, sit here within the doorway, for the night wind is chill; and fill thy pipe."

He came inside as I rose and turned up the lamp so that its light shone full on his bald, bronzed head and deeply tatooed arms and shoulders. Laying down his polished staff of **temana** wood, he came over to me, placed his hand on my arm, patted it gently, and then his kindly old eyes sought mine.

"Be not dull of heart, **taka taina**.[1] A ship will soon come--it may be to-mor-row; it must be soon; for twice have I heard the cocks crow at midnight since I was last here, three days ago. And when the cocks crow at night-time a ship is near."

"May it be so, Pakia, for I am weary of waiting. Ten months have come and gone since I first put foot on this land of Nukufetau, and a ship was to have come here in four."

He filled his pipe, then drawing a small mat near my lounge, he squatted on the floor, and we smoked in silence, listening to the gentle lapping of the lagoon waters upon the inner beach and the beating, never-ceasing hum of the surf on the reef beyond. Overhead the branches of the palms swayed and rustled to the night-breeze.

Presently, as I turned to look seaward, I caught the old man's dark eyes fixed upon my face, and in them I read a sympathy that at that time and place was grateful to me.

"Six months is long for one who waits, Pakia," I said. "I came here but to stay four months and trade for copra; then the ship was to call and take me to Ponape, in the far north-west. And Ponape is a great land to such a man as me."

"*Etonu! Etonu!* I know it. Thrice have I been there when I sailed in the whale-ships. A great land truly, like the island called Juan Fernandez, of which I have told thee, with high mountains green to the summits with trees, and deep, dark valleys wherein the sound of the sea is never heard but when the surf beats hard upon the reef. Ah! a fine land--better than this poor *motu*, which is as but a ring of sand set in the midst of the deep sea. Would that I were young to go there with thee! Tell me, dost know the two small, high islands in the *ava*[2] which is called Jakoits? Hast seen the graves of two white men there?"

"I know the islands well; but I have never seen the graves of any white men there. Who were they, and when did they die?"

"Ah, I am a foolish old man. I forget how old I am. Perhaps, when thou wert a child in thy mother's arms, the graves stood up out of the greensward at the foot of the high cliff which faces to the south. Tell me, is there not a high wall of rock a little way back from the landing beach?... Aye!... that is the place ... and the bones of the men are there, though now great trees may grow over the place. They were both good men--good to look at, tall and strong; and they fought and died there just under the cliff. I saw them die, for I was there with the captain of my ship. We, and others with us, saw it all."

"Who were they, Pakia, and how came they to fight?"

"One was a trader, whose name was Preston; he lived on the mainland of Ponape, where he had a great house and oil store and many servants. The name of the other man was Frank. They fought because of a woman."

"Tell me the story, Pakia. Thou hast seen many lands and many strange things. And when ye come and sit and talk to me the dulness goeth away from me and I no longer think of the ship; for of all the people on this *motu*, to thee and Temana my servant alone do I talk freely. And Temana is now at church."

The old man chuckled. "Aye, he is at church because Malepa, his wife, is so jealous of him that she fears to leave him alone. Better would it please him to be sitting here with us."

I drew the mat curtain across the sitting-room window so that we could not be seen by prying eyes, and put two cups, a gourd of water, and some brandy on the table. Except my own man, Temana, the rest of the natives were intensely jealous of the poor old ex-sailor and wanderer in many lands, and they very much resented his frequent visits to me--partly on account of the occasional glass of grog which I gave him, and partly because he was suspected of still being a *tagata po-uriuri, i.e.*, a heathen. This, however, he vigorously denied, and though Mareko, the Samoan teacher, was a kind-hearted and tolerant man for a native minister, the deacons delighted in persecuting and harassing the ancient upon every possible opportunity, and upon one pretext or another had succeeded in robbing him of his land and dividing it among his relatives; so that now in his extreme old age he was dependent upon one of his daughters, a woman who herself must have been past sixty.

I poured some brandy into the cups; we clicked them together and said, "May you be lucky" to each other. Then he told me of Solepa.

*   *   *   *   *

"There were many whaleships came to anchor in the three harbours of Ponape in those days. They came there for wood and water and fresh provisions, before they sailed to the cold, icy seas of the south. I was then a boat-steerer in an English ship--a good and lucky ship with a good captain. When we came to Ponape we found there six other whaleships, all anchored close together under the shelter of the two islets. All the captains were friends, and the few white men who lived on shore were friends with them, and every night there was much singing and dancing on board the ships, for, as was the custom, every one on board had been given a Ponape girl for wife as long as his ship stayed there; and sometimes a ship would be there a long time--a month perhaps.

"The trader who lived in the big house was one of the first to come on board our ship; for the captain and he were good friends. They talked together on the poop deck, and I heard the trader say that he had been away to Honolulu for nearly a year and had brought back with him a young wife.

"'Good,' said my captain, 'to-night I shall come ashore and drink *manuia!*[3] to ye both.'

"The trader was pleased, and said that some of the other captains could come also, and that he had sent a letter to the other trader, Frank, who lived on the other side of the island, bidding him to come and greet the new wife. At these words the face of Stacey--that was my captain's name, became dark, and he said--

"'You are foolish. Such a man as he is, is better away from thy house--and thy wife. He is a *manaia*, an *ulavale*[4]. Take heed of my words and have no dealings with him.'

"But the man Preston only laughed. He was a fool in this though he was so clever in many other things. He was a big man, broad in the shoulders with the bright eye and the merry laugh of a boy. He had been a sailor, but had wearied of the life, and so he bought land in Ponape and became a trader. He was a fair-dealing man with the people there, and so in three or four years he became rich, and bought more land and built a schooner which he sent away to far distant islands to trade for pearl-shell and *loli* (beche-de-mer). Then it was that he went to Honolulu and came back with a wife.

"That day ere it became dark I went on shore with my captain; some of the other captains went with us. The white man met them on the beach, surrounded by many of his servants, male and female. Some were of Ponape, some from Tahiti, some from Oahu, and some from the place which you call Savage Island and we call Niue. As soon as the captains had stepped out upon the beach and I had bidden the four sailors who were with me to push off to return to the ship, the trader, seeing the tatooing on my arms, gave a shout.

"'Ho,' he cried, turning to my captain, 'whence comes that boat-steerer of thine? By the markings on his arms and chest he should be from the isles of the Tokelau.'

"My captain laughed. 'He comes from near there. He is of Nukufetau.'

"Then let him stay on shore to-night, for there are here with me a man and a woman from Nanomaga; they can talk together. And my wife Solepa, too, will be well pleased to see him, for her mother was a Samoan, and this man can talk to her in her mother's tongue.'

"'So I too went up to the house with the white men, but would not enter with them, for I was stripped to the waist and could not go into the presence of the lady. Presently the man and woman from Nanomaga sought me out and embraced me and made much of me and took me into another part of the house, where I waited till one of my shipmates returned from the ship bringing my jumper and trousers of white duck and a new Panama hat. Ta|pa|! I was a fine-looking man in those days, and women looked at me from the corner of the eye. And now--look at me now! I am like a blind fish which is swept hither and thither by the current against the rocks and sandbanks. Give me some more grog, dear friend; when I talk of the days of my youth my belly yearns for it, and I am not ashamed to beg.

"Presently, after I had dressed myself, I was taken by the Nanomea man into the big room where Solepa, the white man's wife, was sitting with the white men. She came to me and took my hand, and said to me in Samoan 'Talofa, Pakia, e ma|lolo| ea oe?'[5] and my heart was glad; for it was long since I heard any one speak in a tongue which is akin to mine own.... Was she beautiful? you ask. Ta|pa|! All women are beautiful when they are young, and their eyes are full and clear and their voices are soft and their bosoms are round and smooth! All I can remember of her is that she was very young, with a white, fair skin, and dressed like the ***papa-lagi***[6] women I have seen in Peretania and Ita|lia and in Chili and in Sydney.

"As I stood before her, hat in hand and with my eyes looking downward, which is proper and correct for a modest man to do when a high lady speaks to him before many people, a white man who had been sitting at the far end of the room came over to me and said some words of greeting to me. This was Franka[7]--he whom my captain said was a ***manaia***. He was better clothed than any other of the white men, and was proud and overbearing in his manner. He had brought with him more than a score of young Ponape men, all of whom carried rifles and had cutlasses strapped to their waists. This was done to show the people of Jakoits that he was as great a man as Preston, whom he hated, as you will see. But Preston had naught for him but good words, and when he saw the armed men he bade them welcome and set aside a house for them to sleep in, and his servants brought them many baskets of cooked food--taro and yams, and fish, turtle, and pork. All this I saw whilst I was in the big room.

"After I had spoken with the lady Solepa I returned to where the man from Nanomaga and his wife were awaiting me. They pressed me to eat and drink, and by and by sent for a young girl to make kava. Ta|pa|! that kava of Ponape! It is not made there as it is in Samoa--where the young men and women chew the dried root and mix it in a wooden *tanoa* (bowl); there the green root is crushed up in a hollowed stone and but little water is added, so that it is strong, very strong, and one is soon made drunk.

"The girl who made the kava for us was named Sipi. She had eyes like the stars when they are shining upon a deep mountain pool, and round her smooth forehead was bound a circlet of yellow pandanus leaf worked with beads of many colours and fringed with red parrakeet feathers; about her waist were two fine mats, and her bosom and hands were stained with turmeric. I sat and watched her beating the kava, and as her right arm rose and fell her short, black wavy hair danced about her cheeks and hid the red mouth and white teeth when she smiled at me. And she smiled at me very often, and the man and woman beside me laughed when they saw me regard her so intently, and asked me was it in my mind to have her for my wife.

"I did not answer at once, for I knew that if I ran away from the ship for the sake of this girl I would be doing a foolish thing, for I had money coming to me when the ship was *oti folau* (paid off). But, as I pondered, the girl bent forward and again her eyes smiled at me through her hair; and then it was I saw that on her head there was a narrow shaven strip from the crown backward. Now, in Tokelau, this fashion is called *tu tagita*, and showeth that a girl is in her virginity. When I saw this I was pleased, but to make sure I said to my friends, 'Her hair is *tu tagita*. Is she a virgin?'

"The woman of Nanomaga laughed loudly at this and pinched my hand, then she translated my words to the girl who looked into my face and laughed too, shaking her head as she put one hand over her eyes--

"'Nay, nay, O stranger,' she said, 'I am no virgin; neither am I a harlot. I am respectable, and my father and mother have land. I do not go to the ships.' Then she tossed her hair back from her face and began to beat the kava again.

"Now, this girl pleased me greatly, for there were no twists in her tongue; so, when the kava-drinking was finished I made her sit beside me, and the Nanomaga woman told her I would run away from the ship if she would be my wife. She put her face to my shoulder, and then took the circlet from her forehead and bound it round my bared arm, and I gave her a silver ring which I wore on my little finger. Then, together with the Nanomaga man and his wife, we made our plans.... Ah! she was a fine girl. For nearly a year was she wife to me until she sickened and died of the **meisake elo**[8] which was brought to Ponape by the missionary ship from Honolulu.

"So the girl and I made our plans, and my friends promised to hide me when the time came for me to run away. We sat long into the night, and I heard much of the man called Franka and of the jealousy he bore to Preston. He was jealous of him because of two reasons; one was that he possessed such a fine house and so much land and a schooner, and the other was that the people of Jakoits paid him the same respect as they paid one of their high chiefs. So that was why Franka hated him. His heart was full of hatred, and sometimes when he was drunk in his own house at Ro|an Kiti he would boast to the natives that he would one day show them that he was a better man than Preston. Sometimes his drunken boastings were brought to the ears of Preston, who only laughed and took no heed, and always gave him the good word when they met, which was but seldom, for Jakoits and Kiti are far apart, and there was bad blood between the people of the two places. And then--so the girl Sipi afterwards told me--Franka was a lover of grog and a stealer of women, and kept a noisy house and made much trouble, and so Preston went not near him, for he was a quiet man and no drinker, and hated dissension. And, besides this, Franka took part in the wars of the Kiti people, and went about with a following of armed men, and such money as he made in trading he spent in muskets and powder and ball; for all this Preston had no liking, and one day he said to Franka, 'Be warned, this fighting and slaying is wrong; it is not correct for a white man to enter into these wars; you are doing wrong, and some day you will be killed.' Now these were good words, but of what use are good words to an evil heart?

"So we pair sat talking and smoking, and the girl Sipi made us more kava, and then again sat by my side and leant her face against my shoulder, and presently we heard the sounds of music and singing from the big house. We went outside to see and listen, and saw that Preston was playing on a **pese laakau**[9] and Solepa and the captain of my ship were dancing together--like as white people dance--and two of the other captains were also dancing in the same fashion. All round the room were seated many of the high chiefs of Ponape with their wives, dressed very finely, and at one end of the room stood a long table covered with a white cloth, on which was laid food of all kinds and wine and grog to drink--just as you would see in your own country when a rich man gives a feast. Presently as we looked, we saw Franka walk into the room from a side door and look about. His face was flushed, and he staggered slightly in his steps. He went over to the table and poured out some grog, and then beckoned to Preston to come and drink with him, but Preston smiled and shook his head. How could he go when he was making the music? Then Franka struck his clenched fist on the table in anger, and went over to Preston, just as the dancers had stopped.

"'Why will ye not drink with me?' he said in a loud voice so that all heard him. 'Art thou too great a man to drink with me again?'

"'Nay,' answered the other jestingly and taking no heed of Franka's rude voice and angry eyes, 'not so great that I cannot drink with all my friends tonight, be they white or brown,' and so saying he bade every one in the room come to the great table with him and drink *manuia* to him and his young wife.

"So the nine white men--Preston, and Franka, and the seven whaleship captains, and Nanakin, the head chief of Ponape, and many other lesser chiefs, all gathered together around the table and filled their glasses and drank *manuia* to the bride, who sat on a chair in the centre of the room surrounded by the chiefs' wives, and smiled and bowed when my captain called her name and raised his glass towards her. Then after this he again took up the *pese laakau* and began to play, and my captain and Solepa danced again. Suddenly Franka pushed his way through the others and rudely placed his hand on her arm.

"'Come,' he said, 'leave this fellow and dance with me.'

"She cried out in terror, and then silence fell upon all as my captain withdrew his right arm from her waist and struck Franka on the mouth; it was a strong blow, and Franka staggered backwards and then fell near to the open door. As he rose to his feet again my captain came up to him and bade him leave quickly. 'We want no drunken bullies here,' he said, and at that moment Franka drew a pistol and pointed it at his chest. I leapt upon him and as we struggled together the pistol went off, but the bullet hurt no one.

"Then there was a great commotion, and my captain and Preston ran to my aid and seized Franka. They dragged him out of the room, and with words of scorn and contempt threw him out amongst his own people who were gathered together outside the house, with their muskets in their hands. But already Nanakin and his chiefs had summoned their fighting men; they came running towards us from all directions, and surrounding Franka and his men, drove them away and bade them beware of ever returning to Jakoits.

"When they had gone, my captain called me to him, and, turning to the other white men, said, 'This man hath saved my life. He hath a brave heart. I shall do much for him in the time to come.' Then he and the others all shook my hand and praised me, and I was silent and said nothing, for I was ashamed to think I was about to run away from such a good captain.

"In the morning we went back to the ship, and the boats were then sent away to fill and bring off casks of water. Every time my boat went I took something with me; tobacco and clothing and other things which I had in my sea chest. Sipi and some other girls met us at the watering place, and they took these from me and put them in a place of safety. That afternoon as the boats were about to leave the shore for the last time, towing the casks, I slipped into the forest which grew very densely on both sides of the little river, and ran till I came to the spot where Sipi was awaiting me. Then together we went inland towards the mountains and kept on walking till nightfall. That night we slept in the forest; we were afraid to make a fire lest it should be seen by some of Nanakin's people and betray us, for I knew that my captain would cause a great search to be made for me. When dawn came we again set out and went on steadily till we came to the summit of the range of mountains which divides the island. There was a clear space on the side of the mountain; a great village had once stood there, so Sipi told me, but all those who had dwelt there had long since died, and their ghosts could be heard flitting to and fro at night time. Far below us we could see the blue sea, and the long waving line of reef with the surf beating upon it, and within, anchored in the green water, were the seven ships and Preston's schooner.

"All that day and the next the girl and I worked at building a little house for us to live in until the ships had gone. We had no fear of any one seeking us out in that place, for it had a bad name and none but travelling parties from Ro|an Kiti ever passed there. Sipi had brought with her a basket of cooked food; in the deserted plantations we found plenty of bananas and yams, and in the stream at the foot of the valley we caught many small fish. Four days went by, and then one morning we saw the ships set their sails and go to sea. We watched them till they touched the sky rim and disappeared; then we went back to Jakoits.

"The white man and Solepa were sitting under the shade of a tree in front of their house. I went boldly up to him and asked him to give me work to do. At first he was angry, for he and my captain were great friends, and said he would have naught to do with me. Why did I run away from such a good man and such a good ship? There were too many men like me, he said, in Ponape, who had run away so that they might do naught but wander from village to village and eat and drink and sleep. Then again he asked why I had run away.

"'Because of her,' I said, pointing to the girl Sipi, who was sitting at the gate with her face covered with the corner of her mat. 'But I am no *tafao vale*.[10] I am a true man. Give me work on thy ship.'

"He thought a little while, then he and Solepa talked together, and Solepa bade Sipi come near so that she might talk to her. Presently he said to me that I had done a foolish thing to run away for the sake of the girl when I had money coming to me and when the captain's heart was filled with friendship towards me for turning aside Franka's pistol.

"I bent my head, for I was ashamed. Then I said, 'I care not for the money I have lost, but I am eaten up with shame for running away, for my captain was a good captain to me.'

"This pleased him, for he smiled and said, 'I will try thee. I will make thee boatswain of the schooner, and this girl here shall be servant to my wife.'

"So Sipi became servant to Solepa, and I was sent on board the schooner to help prepare her for sea. My new captain gave us a house to live in, and every night I came on shore. Ah, those were brave times, and Preston made much of me when he found that I was a true man and did my work well, and would stand no saucy words nor black looks from those of the schooner's crew who thought that the boatswain should be a white man.

"Ten days after the whaleships had sailed, the schooner was ready for sea. We were to sail to the westward isles to trade for oil and tortoiseshell, and then go to China, where Preston thought to sell his cargo. On the eve of the day on which we were to leave, the mate, who was an old and stupid Siamani,[11] went ashore to my master's house, and I was left in charge of the schooner. Sipi, my wife, was with me, and we sat together in the stern of the ship, smoking our *sului* (cigarettes) and talking of the time when I should return and buy a piece of land from her father's people, on which I should build a new house. There were six native sailors on board, and these, as the night drew on, spread their mats on the fore deck and went to sleep. Then Sipi and I went into the cabin, which was on deck, and we too slept.

"How long we had slumbered I cannot tell, but suddenly we were aroused by the sound of a great clamour on deck and the groans and cries of dying men, and then ere we were well awakened the cabin door was opened and Solepa was thrust inside. Then the door was quickly closed and fastened on the outside, and I heard Franka's voice calling out orders to hoist sails and slip the cable.

"There was a lamp burning dimly in the cabin, and Sipi and I ran to the aid of Solepa, who lay prone upon the floor as if dead. Her dress was torn, and her hands and arms were scratched and bleeding, so that Sipi wept as she leant over her and put water to her lips. In a little while she opened her eyes, and when she saw us a great sob broke from her bosom and she caught my hand in hers and tried to speak.

"Now, grog is a good thing. It is good for a weak, panting woman when her strength is gone and her soul is terrified, and it is good for an old man who is despised by his relations because he is bitten with poverty. There was grog in a wicker jar in the cabin. I gave her some in a glass, and then as the dog Franka, whose soul and body are now in hell, was getting the schooner under way, she told me that while she and Preston were asleep the house was surrounded by a hundred or more of men from Ro|an Kiti, led by Franka. They burst in suddenly, and Franka and some others rushed into their sleeping-room and she was torn away from her husband and carried down to the beach.

"'Is thy husband dead?' I asked.

"'I cannot tell,' she said in a weak voice. 'I heard some shots fired and saw him struggling with Franka's men. That is all I know. If he is dead then shall I die too. Give me a knife, so that I may die.'

"As she spoke the schooner began to move, and again we heard Franka's voice calling out in English to some one to go forward and con the ship whilst he steered, for the night was dark and he, clever stealer of women as he was, did not know the passage out through the reef, and trusted to those with him who knew but little more. Then something came into my mind, and I took Solepa's hand in mine.

"'I will save thee from this pig Franka,' I said quickly, 'he shall never take thee away. Sit ye here with Sipi, and when ye hear the schooner strike, spring ye both into the sea and swim towards the two islands which are near.'

"In the centre of the deck cabin was a hatch which led into the hold. There was no deck between, for the vessel was but small. I took my knife from the sheath and then lifted the hatch, descended, and crawled forward in the darkness to the fore hatch, up which I crept very carefully, for I had much in my mind. I saw a man standing up, holding on to the fore stay. He was calling out to Franka every now and then, telling him how to steer. I sprang up behind him, and as I drove my knife into his back with my left hand, I struck him with my right on his neck and he fell overboard. He was a white man, I think for when my knife went into his back he called out 'Oh Christ!' But then many native men who have mixed with white people call out 'Oh, Christ,' just like white men when they are drunk. Anyway, it does not matter now.

"But as I struck my knife into him, I called out in English to put the helm hard down, for I saw that the schooner was very near the reef on the starboard hand. Franka, who was at the wheel, at once obeyed and was fooled, for the schooner, which was now leaping and singing to the strong night wind from the mountains smote suddenly upon the coral reef with a noise like the felling of a great forest tree, and began to grind and tear her timbers.

"Almost as she struck Solepa and Sipi stood by me, and together we sprang overboard into the white surf ... Give me some more grog, dear friend of my heart. I am no boaster, nor am I a liar; but when I think of that swim to the shore through the rolling seas with those two women, my belly cleaves to my backbone and I become faint.... For the current was against us, and neither Sipi nor Solepa were good swimmers, and many times had we to clutch hold of the jagged coral, which tore our skins so that our blood ran out freely, and had the sharks come to us then I would not be here with thee to-night drinking this, thy good sweet grog which thou givest me out of thy kind heart. Ta|pa|! When I look into thy face and see thy kind eyes, I am young again. I love thee, not alone because thou hast been kind to me in my poverty and paid the fines of my granddaughter when she hath committed adultery with the young men of the village, but because thou hast seen many lands and have upheld me before the teacher, who is a circumcised but yet unta-tooed dog of a Samoan. A man who is not tatooed is no better than a woman. He is a male harlot and should be despised. He is only fit to associate with women, and has no right to beget children....

"We three swam to the shore, and when the dawn came we saw that the schoo-ner stood high and dry on the reef and that Franka and his men were trying to float her by throwing overboard the iron ballast and putting a kedge anchor out upon the lee side of the reef. And at the same time we saw three boats put off from the mainland. These boats were all painted white, and when I saw them I said to Solepa, 'Be of good heart. Thy husband is not dead, for here are three of his boats coming. He is not dead. He is coming to seek thee.'"

"The three boats came quickly towards the schooner, but ere they reached her Franka and those with him got into the boats in which they had boarded the ves-sel, and then we saw smoke arise from the bow and stern.... They had set fire to the ship. They were cowards. Fire is a great help to cowards, because in the glare and dazzling light of burning houses or ships, when the thunder of cannons and the rattle of rifles is heard, they can run about and kill people.... I have seen these things done in Chili.... I have seen men who would not stand and fight on board ship run away on shore and slay women and children in their fury and cowardice. No, they were not Englishmen; they were Spaniolas. But the officers were Englishmen and Germans. *They* did not run away, they were killed. Brave men get killed and cow-ards live. I am no coward though I am still alive. It is quite proper that I should live, for I never ran away when there was fighting to be done. I have only been a fool because of my love for women. No one could say I was a coward, and no one can say I am a fool, because I am too old now to be a fool.

"As Franka and those with him left the burning schooner and rowed towards the islands, the three boats from the shore changed their course and followed him. Franka and his men were the first to reach the land, and they quickly ran up the beach and crouched behind the bushes which grew at high-water mark. They all had guns, and Sipi and Solepa and I saw them waiting to shoot. We were hiding amid the roots of a great banyan tree, and could see well. As the boats drew near Solepa watched them eagerly, and then began to weep and laugh at the same time when she saw her husband Preston was steering the one which led. She was a good woman. She loved her husband. I was pleased with her, and told her to be of good cheer, for I was sure that Preston and his people would kill Franka and those with him, for as they rowed they made no noise. No one shouted nor challenged; they came on and on, and the white man Preston stood up with the steer oar in his hand, and his face was as a stone in which was set eyes of fire. When his boat was within twenty fathoms of the beach the rowers ceased, and he held up his hand to those who awaited his coming.

"'Listen to me, men of Ro|an Kiti. We are as three to one of ye, and ye are caught in a trap. Death is in my mouth if I speak the word. Tell me, is my wife Solepa alive?'

"No one answered, but suddenly Franka stepped out from behind the bushes and pointed his rifle at him, and was about to pull the trigger when a young man of his party who was of good heart seized him by the arm, and cried out 'twas a coward's act; then two or three followed him, and together they bore Franka down upon the sand; and one of them cried out to Preston--

"'This is a wrong business. We were led astray by this man. We are no cowards, and have no ill-will to thee. Thy wife is alive. She swam ashore with two others when the ship struck. Are we dead men?'

"Then, ere Preston could answer, Solepa leapt out from beneath the banyan tree and ran through the men of Ro|an Kiti towards the beach, and cried--

"'Oh, my husband, for the love of God let no blood be shed! I am well and un-harmed. Spare these people and spare even this man Franka, for he is mad!'

"Then Preston leapt out of the boat and put his arms around her waist and kissed her, and then put her aside, and called to every one around him--

"'These are my words,' he said. 'I am a man of peace, but this man Franka is a robber and a dog, and hath stolen upon me in the night and slain my people, and his hands are reddened with blood. And he hath put foul dishonour on me by stealing Solepa my wife, and carrying her away from my house as if she were a slave or a harlot. And there is no room here for such a man to live unless he be a better man than I. But I am no murderer. So stand aside all! Let him rise and rest awhile, and then shall we two fight, man to man. Either he or I must die.'

"Then many men of both sides came to him and said, 'Let this thing be finished.

You are a strong man. Take this robber and slay him as you would slay a pig.' But he put them aside, and said he would fight him man to man, as Englishmen fought.

"So when Franka was rested two cutlasses were brought, and the two men stood face to face on the sand. I kept close to Franka, for I meant to stab him if I could, but Preston angrily bade me stand back. Then the two crossed their swords together and began to fight. It was a great fight, but it did not last long, for Preston soon ran his sword through Franka's chest. I saw it come out through his back. But as he fell and Preston bent over him he thrust his cutlass into Preston's stomach and worked it to and fro. Then Preston fell on him, and they died together.

"There was no more bloodshed. Solepa and Sipi and I dressed the dead man in his best clothes, and the Ro|an Kiti men dressed Franka in his best clothes, and a great funeral feast was made, and we buried them together on the little island. And Solepa went back again to Honolulu in a whaleship. She was young and fair, and should have soon found another husband. I do not know. But Sipi was a fine wife to me."

The Fisher Folk of Nukufetau

Early one morning, about a week after I had settled down on Nukufetau as a trader, I opened my chest of fishing-gear and began to overhaul it. In a few minutes I was surrounded by an eager and interested group of natives, who examined everything with the greatest curiosity.

Now for the preceding twelve months I had been living on the little island of Nanomaga, a day's sail from Nukufetau; and between Nanomaga and Nukufetau there was a great bitterness of long standing--the Nanomagans claimed to be the most daring canoe-men and expert fishermen in all the eight isles of the Ellice Group, and the people of Nukufetau resented the claim strongly. The feeling had been accentuated by my good friend the Samoan teacher on Nanomaga, himself an ardent fisherman, writing to his brother minister on Nukufetau and informing him that although I was not a high-class Christian I was all right in all other respects, and a good fisherman--"all that he did not know we have taught him, therefore," he added slyly, "let your young men watch him so that they may learn how to fish in deep and rough water, such as ours." These remarks were of course duly made public, and caused much indignation, neither the minister nor his flock liking the gibe about the deep, rough water; also the insinuation that anything about fishing was to be learnt from the new white man was annoying and uncalled for.

I must here mention that the natives of De Peyster's Island (Nukufetau) caught all the fish they wanted in the smooth and spacious waters of the lagoon, and were not fond of venturing outside the barrier reef, except during the bonito season, or when the sea was very calm at night, to catch flying-fish. Then, too, the currents outside the reef were swift and dangerous, and the canoes had either to be carried a long distance over the coral or paddled a couple of miles across the lagoon to the ship passage before the open sea was gained. Hudson's Island (Nanomaga)--a tiny spot less than four miles in circumference--had no lagoon, and all fishing was done in the deep water of the ocean. The natives were used to launching their canoes, year in and year out, to face the wildest surf, and were, in consequence, wonderfully expert, and in the history of the island there is only one instance of a man having been drowned. The De Peyster people, by reason of the advantage of their placid lagoon, had no reason to risk their lives in the surf in this manner, and so, naturally enough, they were not nearly as skilful in the management of their frail canoes when they had to face a sweeping sea on the outer or ocean reef.

Just as I was placing some coils of heavy, deep-sea lines upon the matted floor, Mareko the native teacher, fat, jovial, and bubbling-voiced, entered in a great hurry, and hardly giving himself time to shake hands with me, announced in a tone of triumph, that a body of *atuli* (baby bonito) had just entered the passage and were making their way up the lagoon.

In less than ten seconds every man, woman, and child on the island, except the teacher and myself, were agog with excitement and bawling and shouting as they rushed to the beach to launch and man the canoes, the advent of the *atuli* having been expected for some days. In nearly all the equatorial islands of the Pacific these beautiful little fish make their appearance every year almost to a day, with unvarying regularity. They remain in the smooth waters of lagoons for about two weeks, swimming about in incredible numbers, and apparently so terrified of their many enemies in their own element, and the savage, keen-eyed frigate birds which constantly assail them from above, that they sometimes crowd into small pools on the inner reef, and when the tide is low, seek to hide themselves by lying in thick masses under the overhanging ledges of coral rock. Simultaneously--or at least within a day or two at most--the swarming millions of *atuli* are followed into the lagoons by the *gatala*--a large black and grey rock-cod (much esteemed by the natives for the delicacy of its flavour) and great numbers of enormous eels. At other times of the year both the *gatala* and the eels are never or but rarely seen inside the lagoons, but are occasionally caught outside the reef at a good depth-- forty to sixty fathoms. As soon, however, as the young bonito appear, both eels and rock-cod change their normal habits, and entering the lagoons through the passages thereto, they take up their quarters in the deeper parts--places which are fringed by a labyrinthine border of coral forest, and are at most ten fathoms deep. Here, when the *atuli* are covering the surface above, the eels and rock-cod actually rise to the surface and play havoc among them, especially during moonlight nights, and in the daytime both rock-cod and eels may be seen pursuing their hapless prey in the very shallowest water, amidst the little pools and runnels of the coral reef. It is at this time that the natives of Nukufetau and some other islands have some glorious sport, for in addition to the huge eels and rock-cod many other deep-sea fish flock into the shallower lagoon waters--all in pursuit of the *atuli*--and all eager to take the hook.

*   *   *   *   *

As soon as the natives had left the house, Mareko turned to me with a beaming smile. "Let them go on first and net some *atuli* for us for bait," he said, "you and I shall follow in my own canoe and fish for *gatala*. It will be a great thing for one of us to catch the first *gatala* of the season. Yesterday, when I was over there," pointing to two tiny islets within the lagoon, "I saw some *gatala*. The natives laugh at me and say I am mistaken--that because the *atuli* had not come there could be no *gatala*. Now, *I* think that the big fish came in some days ago, but the strong wind and current kept the *atuli* outside till now. Come."

I needed no pressing. In five minutes I had my basket of lines (of white American cotton) ready, and joined Mareko. His canoe (the best on the island, of course) was already in the water and manned by his two sons, boys of eight and twelve respectively. I sat for'ard, the two youngsters amidships, the father took the post of honour as *tautai* or steersman, and with a chuckle of satisfaction from the boys, off we went in the wake of about thirty other canoes.

Oh, the delight of urging a light canoe over the glassy water of an island lagoon, and watching the changing colours and strange, grotesque shapes of the coral trees and plants of the garden beneath as they vanish swiftly astern, and the quick *chip, chip* of the flashing paddles sends the whirling, noisy eddies to right and left, and frights the lazy, many-hued rock-fish into the darker depths beneath! On, on, till the half mile or more of shallow water which covers the inner reef is passed, and then suddenly you shoot over the top of the submarine wall, into deepest, loveliest blue, full thirty fathoms deep, and as calm and quiet as an infant sleeping on its mother's bosom, though perhaps not a quarter of a mile away on either hand the long rollers of the Pacific are bellowing and thundering on the grim black shelves of the weather coast.

So it was on this morning, but with added delights and beauties; as instead of striking straight across the lagoon to our rendezvous we had to skirt the beaches of a chain of thickly wooded islets, which gave forth a sweet smell, mingled with the odours of ***nono*** blossoms; for during the night rain had fallen after a long month of dry weather, and Nature was breathing with joy. High overhead there floated some snow-white tropic birds--those gentle, ethereal creatures which, to the toil-spent seaman who watches their mysterious poise in illimitable space, seem to denote the greater Mystery and Rest that lieth beyond all things; and lower down, and sweeping swiftly to and fro with steady, outspread wing and long, forked tail, the fierce-eyed, savage frigate birds scanned the surface of the water in search of prey, and then finding it not, rose without apparent motion to the cloudless canopy of blue and became as but tiny black specks--and then, ***swish***! and the tiny black specks which but a minute ago were high in heaven are flashing by your cheeks with a weird, whistling sound like winged spectres. You look for them. They are gone. Already they are a thousand feet overhead. Five of them. And all five are as motionless as if they, with their wide, outspread wings, had never moved from their present position for a thousand years.

"Chip, chip," and "chunk, chunk," go our paddles as we now head eastward towards the rising sun in whose resplendent rays the tufted palms of the two islets stand clearly out, silhouetted against the sea rim beyond. Now and again we hear, as from a long, long distance, the echoes of the voices of the people in the canoes ahead; a soft white mist began to gather over and then ascend from the water, and as we drew near the islets the occasional thunder of the serf on Motuluga Reef we heard awhile ago changed into a monotonous droning hum.

"***Aue***!" said Mareko the ***tautai***, with a laugh, as he ceased paddling and laid his paddle athwartships, "'tis like to be a hot day and calm. So much the better for our fishing, for the water will be very clear. Boy, give me a coconut to drink."

"Take some whisky with it, Mareko," I said, taking a flask out of my basket.

"***Isa***! Shame upon you! How can you say such a thing to me, a minister!" And then he added, with a reproachful look, "and my children here, too." He would have winked, but he dared not do so, for one of his boys had turned his face aft and was facing him. I, however, made him a hurried gesture which he quite understood. Good old Mareko! He was an honest, generous-hearted, broad-minded fellow, but terribly afraid of his tyrannical deacons, who objected to him smoking even in the seclusion of his own curatage, and otherwise bullied and worried him into behaving exactly as they thought he should.

By the time we reached the islets the *atuli* catching had begun, and more than a hundred natives were encircling a considerable area of water with finely-meshed nets and driving the fish shoreward upon a small sandy beach, where they were scooped up in gleaming masses of shining blue and silver by a number of women and children, who tumbled over and pushed each other aside amidst much laughter and merriment.

On the larger of the two islets were a few thatched huts with open sides. One of these was reserved for the missionary and the white man, and hauling our canoe up on the beach at the invitation of the people, we sat down under a shed whilst the women grilled us some of the freshly-caught fish. This took barely over ten minutes, as fires had already been lighted by the children. The absence of bread was made up for by the flesh of half-grown coconuts and cooked *puraka*--gigantic species of taro which thrives well in the sandy soil of the Equatorial islands of the Pacific. Just as we had finished eating and were preparing our lines we heard loud cries from the natives who were still engaged among the *atuli*, and three or four of them seizing spears began chasing what were evidently some large fish. Presently one of them darted his weapon, and then gave a loud cry of triumph, as he leapt into the water and dragged out a large salmon-like fish called "utu", which was at once brought ashore for my inspection. The man who had struck it--an active, wiry old fellow named Viliamu (William) was panting with excitement. Some large *gatala*, he said, had just made their appearance with the *utu* and were pursuing the small fish; therefore would we please hurry forward with our preparations. Then the leader of the entire party stood up and bellowed out in bull-like tones his instructions. The canoes were all to start together, and when the ground was reached all lines were to be lowered simultaneously; there was to be no crowding. The white man and missionary, however, if they wished, could start first and make a choice of position.

"No, no," I said, "let us all start fair."

This was greeted with a chorus of approval, and then leaving the women and children to attend to the camp, we hurried back to the canoes. Just as we were leaving the hut I had a look at the **utu**--a fish I had never before seen. It was about three feet in length, and only for its head (which was coarse and clumsy) much like a heavy salmon. The back was covered with light green scales, the sides and belly a pure silver, and the fins and tail tipped with yellow. It weighed about 20 lbs., and presented a very handsome appearance.

The fishing-ground to which we were now paddling was not half a mile from the islets, and lay between them and the outer reef which formed its northern boundary. It consisted of a series of deep channels or connected pools running or situated amidst a network of minor reefs, the surfaces of which were, for the most part, bare at low water. Generally the depth was from eight to ten fathoms; in places, however, it was much deeper, and I subsequently found that there were spots whereon I could stand (on the coral ledge) and drop my line into chasms of thirty-two or thirty-three fathoms. Here the water was almost as blue to the eye as the ocean, and here the very largest fish resorted--such as the **pura**, a species of rock-cod, and a blue-scaled groper, the native name of which I cannot now recall.

It must have been nearly ten o'clock when the canoes were all in position, and the word was given to let go lines. The particular spot in which we were congregated was about three acres in extent and about seven fathoms in depth, with water as clear as crystal; and even the dullest eye could discern the smallest pebble or piece of broken coral lying upon the bottom, which was generally composed of patches of coarse sand surrounded by an interlacing fringe of growing coral, or white, blue, or yellow boulders. A glance over the side showed us that the **gatala** had arrived; we could see numbers of them swimming lazily to and fro beneath, awaiting the flowing tide which would soon cover the lagoon from one shore to the other with swarms of young bonito, as they swam about in search of such places as that in which we were now about to begin fishing.

Each man had baited his hook with the third of an **atuli**--at this stage of their life about four inches long and exactly the colour and shape of a young mackerel-- and within five minutes after "**Tu'u tau kafa**!" ("Let go lines!") had been called out several of the canoes around our own began to pull up fish--four to six pounders. I was fishing with a white cotton line, with two hooks, and Mareko with the usual native gear--a hand-made line of hibiscus bark with a barbless hook made from a long wire nail, with its point ground fine and well-curved inwards. We both struck fish at the same moment, and I knew by the zigzag pull that I had two. Up they came together--three spotted beauties about eighteen inches in length and weighing over 5 lbs. each. Then I found the advantage of the native style of hook; Mareko simply put his left thumb and forefinger into the fish's eye, had his hook free in a moment, had baited, lowered again and was pulling up another before I had succeeded in freeing even my first hook which was firmly fixed in the fish's gullet, out of sight. I soon put myself on a more even footing by cutting off the small one and a half inch hooks I had been using and bending on two thick and long-shanked four inchers. These answered beautifully, as although the barbs caused me some trouble, their stout shanks afforded a good grip and leverage when extracting them from the hard and keen-toothed jaws of the struggling fish. Then, too, I had another advantage over my companions; I was wearing a pair of seaboots which effectually protected my feet from either the terrible fins or the teeth of the fish in the bottom of the canoe.

I had caught my eighth fish, when an outcry came from a canoe near us, as a young man who was seated on the for'ard thwart rose to his feet and began hauling in his line, which was standing straight up and down, taut as an iron bar, the canoe meanwhile spinning round and round although the steersman used all his efforts to keep her steady.

"What is it, Tuluia?" called out fifty voices at once. "A shark?"

"My mother's bones!" said old Viliamu with a laugh of contempt. "'Tis an eel, and Tuluia, who was asleep, has let it twist its tail around a piece of coral. May he lose it for his stupidity."

We all ceased fishing to watch, and half a dozen men began jeering at the lad, who was too excited to heed them. Old Viliamu, who was in the next canoe, looked down, and then cried out that he could see the eel, which had taken several turns of its body around a thick branch of growing coral.

"His head is up," he called out to the youth, "but you cannot move him, he has too many turns in and out among the coral." Then paddling up alongside he again looked at the struggling creature, then felt the line which was vibrating with the tension. Stepping out of his own craft into that of the young man, the line was placed in his hands without an inch of it being payed out, for once one of these giant eels can get his head down he will so quickly twine the line in and out among the rugged coral that it is soon chafed through, if of ordinary thickness. But the ancient knew his work well, as we were soon to see. Taking a turn of the line well up on his forearm and grasping it with his right a yard lower down, he waited for a second or two, then suddenly bent his body till his face nearly touched the water, then he sprang erect and with lightning-like rapidity began to haul in hand *under* hand [12] amid loud cries of approval as the wriggling body of the eel was seen ascending clear of the coral. The moment it reached the surface, a second native, with unerring aim sent a spear through it and then a blow or two upon the head with a club carried for the purpose took all further fight out of the creature, which was then lifted out of the water and dropped into the canoe. Here the end of its tail was quickly split open and we saw no more of him for the time being.

To capture an eel so soon was looked upon as a lucky omen, to have lost it would have been a presage of ill-fortune for the rest of the day, and the incident put every one in high good humour. By this time the tide was flowing over the flatter parts of the reef and young bonito could be seen jumping out of the water in all directions. Immense bodies were, so I was assured by the natives, now coming into the lagoon from the sea, and would continue to do so till the tide turned, when those in the passage, unable to face a six-knot current, would be carried out again, to make another attempt later on.

By this time every canoe was hauling in large rock-cod almost as quick as the lines could be baited, and the bottom of our own craft presented a gruesome sight--a lather of blood and froth and kicking fish, some of which were over 20 lbs. weight. Telling the two boys to cease fishing awhile and stun some of the liveliest, I unthinkingly began to bale out some of the ensanguined water, when a score of indignant voices bade me cease. Did I want to bring all the sharks in the world around us? I was asked; and old Viliamu, who was a sarcastic old gentleman, made a mock apology for me--

"How should he know any better? The sharks of Tokelau have no teeth, like the people there, for they too are eaters of *fala*."

This evoked a sally of laughter, in which of course I joined. I must explain that the natives of the Tokelau Group, among whom I had lived, through constantly chewing the tough drupes of the fruit of the *fala* (pandanus palm) wear out their teeth prematurely, and are sometimes termed "toothless" by other natives of the South Pacific. However, I was to have my own little joke at Viliamu's expense later on.

Just at this time a sudden squall, accompanied by torrents of rain, came down upon us from the eastward, and whilst Mareko and his boys kept us head to wind--none of the canoes were anchored--I took the opportunity of getting ready two of my own lines, each treble-hooked, for the boys. Their own were old and rotten, and had parted so often that they were now too short to be of use, and, besides that, the few remaining hooks of soft wire were too small. As soon as the squall was over I showed Mareko what I had done. He nodded and smiled, but said I should try and break off the barbs--his boys did not understand them as well as native-made hooks. This was quickly accomplished with a heavy knife, and the youngsters began to haul up fish two and three at a time at such a rate that the canoe soon became deep in the water outside and very full inside.

"A few more, Mareko," I said, "and then we'll go ashore, unload, and come back again. I want to tease that old man."

We caught all we could possibly carry in another quarter of an hour, and I was confident that our take exceeded that of any other canoe. This was because the natives would carefully watch their stone sinkers descend, and use every care to keep them from being entangled in the coral, whilst my line, which had a 12 oz. leaden sinker, would plump quickly to the bottom in the midst of the hungry fish; consequently, although I lost some hooks by fouling and now and then dragged up a bunch of coral, I was catching more fish than any one else. And I was not going to let my reputation suffer for the sake of a few hooks. So we coiled up our lines on the outrigger platform, and taking up our paddles headed shoreward, taking care to pass near Viliamu's canoe. He hailed me and asked me for a pipe of tobacco.

"I shall give it to you when we return," I said.

"When you return! Why, where are you going?" he asked.

"On shore, you silly old woman! I have been showing these boys how to fish for *gatala*, and we go because the canoe is sinking. When we return these two *tamariki* (infants) shall show *you* how to fish now that they have learnt from me."

There was a loud laugh at this, and as the old man took the jest very good-naturedly I brought up alongside, showed him our take, and gave him a stick of tobacco. The astonishment of himself and his crew of three at the quantity of fish we had afforded me much satisfaction, though I could not help feeling that our luck was not due to my own skill alone.

Returning to the islets we were just in time to escape two fierce squalls, which lasted half an hour and raised such a sea that the remaining canoes began to follow us, as they were unable to keep on the ground. During our absence the women and children had been most industrious; the weather-worn, dilapidated huts had been made habitable with freshly-plaited *kapaus*--coarse mats of green coconut leaves, the floors covered with clean white pebbles, sleeping mats in readiness, and heaps of young drinking nuts piled up in every corner, whilst outside smoke was arising from a score of ground ovens in which taro and puraka were being cooked, together with bundles of *atuli* wrapped in leaves.

Etiquette forbade Mareko and myself counting our fish until the rest of the party returned, although the women had taken them out of the canoe and laid them on the beach, where the pouring rain soon washed them clean and showed them in all their shining beauty. Among them were two or three parrot-fish--rich carmine, striped with bands of bright yellow, boneless fins, and long protruding teeth in the upper jaw showing out from the thick, fleshy lips; and one *afulu*--a species of deep-water sand mullet with purple scales and yellow fins.

Whilst awaiting the rest of the canoes I drew the teacher into our hut and pressed him to take some whisky. He was wet, cold, and shivering, but resolutely declined to take any. "I should like to drink a little," he said frankly, "but I must not. I cannot drink it in secret, and yet I must not set a bad example. Do not ask me, please. But if you like to give some to the old men do so, but only a very little." I did do so. As soon as the rest of the party landed I called up four of the oldest men and gave each of them a stiff nip. They were all nude to the waist, and like all Polynesians who have been exposed to a cold rain squall, were shivering and miserable. After each man had taken his nip and emitted a deep sigh of satisfaction I observed that hundreds of old white men saved their lives by taking a glass of spirits when they were wet through--they had to do so by the doctor's orders.

"That is true," said one old fellow; "when men grow old, and the rain falls upon them it does not run off their skins as it would from the smooth skins of young men. It gets into the wrinkles and stays there. But when the belly is warmed with grog a man does not feel the cold."

"True," I said gravely, as I poured some whisky out for myself; "true, quite true, my dear friends. And in these islands it is very bad for an old man to be exposed to much rain. That is why I am disturbed in my mind. See, there is Mareko, your minister. He, like you, is old; he is wet and cold. And he shivers. And he will not take a mouthful of this *rom* because he fears scandal. Now if he should become ill and die I should be a disgraced man. This *rom* is now not *rom*; it is medicine. And Mareko should take some even as you have taken it--to keep away danger."

The four old fellows arose to the occasion. They talked earnestly together for a minute, and then formed themselves into a committee, requested me to head them as a deputation with the whisky, and then waited upon their pastor, who was putting on a dry shirt in another hut. I am glad to say that under our united protests he at last consented to save his life, and felt much better.

Presently the women announced that the ovens were ready to be opened. As soon as the fish were counted, and the rain having ceased, we all gathered round the canoes and watched each one emptied of its load. As I imagined, our party had taken the most fish, and not only the most, but the heaviest as well. Mareko added to my blushing honours by informing the company that as a fisherman and a knowledgable man generally I justified his brother minister's opinion and would prove an acquisition to the community. We then inspected the first eel caught, and a truly huge creature it was, quite nine feet in length, and in girth at its thickest part, as near as I could guess with a piece of line, thirty inches. The line with which it was caught was made of new four-stranded coir-cinnet, as thick as a stout lead pencil, and the hook a piece of 3/6 or 1/2 inch iron with a 6-inch shank, once used as a fish spear, without a barb! The natives seemed much pleased at the interest displayed, and told me that sometimes these eels grew to *elua gafa* (*i.e.*, two fathoms), but were seldom caught, and asked me if I had tackle strong enough for such. Later on I showed them a 27-stranded American cotton line 100 fathoms long, with a 4-inch hook, curved in the shank, as thick as a pencil, and "eyed" for a twisted wire snooding. They had never seen such beautiful tackle before, and were loud in their expressions of admiration, but thought the line too thin for a very heavy fish. I told them that at Nanomaga I had caught *palu* (a nocturnal feeding fish of great size) in over sixty fathoms with that same line.

"That is true," said one of them politely, "we were told that you and Tiaki (one Jack O'Brien, an old trader) of Funafuti have caught many *palu* with your long lines; but the *palu* is a weak fish even when he is a fathom long. And as he comes up he grows weaker and weaker, and sometimes he bursts open when he comes to the surface. Now if a big eel--an eel two fathoms long--"

"If he was three fathoms long he could not break this line," I replied positively.

They laughed and told me that when I hooked even a small eel, one half a fathom in length, I would change my opinion.

Soon after our midday meal was over, and we were preparing to return to our fishing-ground with an ample supply of fresh bait, the sky to windward became black and threatening, and through the breaks in the long line of palms on the weather side of the island, which permitted the horizon to be viewed, we could see that a squall of unusual violence was coming. All the canoes were at once hauled up on the lee-side of the islets, the huts were secured by ropes as quickly as possible, and every one hurried under shelter. In a few minutes the wind was blowing with astonishing fury, and the air was full of leaves, sticks, and other *debris*, whilst the coco-palms and other trees on the islets seemed likely to be torn up by the roots. This lasted about ten minutes. Then came a sudden lull, followed by a terrific and deafening downpour of rain; then more wind, another downpour, and the sun was out again!

As soon as the squall was over, I walked round to the weather side of the islet with some children. We found the beach covered with some thousands of *atuli* and beautiful little garfish which had been driven on shore by the force of the wind. We were soon joined by women carrying baskets, which they filled with fish and carried back to the camp. On returning, we again launched the canoes and started off again--to meet with some disappointment, for although the *gatala* still bit freely and several eels were also taken, some scores of the small, pestilent, lagoon sharks were swimming about and played havoc with our lines. These torments are from two to four feet in length, and their mouths, which are quite out of proportion to their insignificant size, are set with rows of teeth of razor-like keenness. The moment a baited hook was seen one of these little wretches would dart at it like lightning, and generally bit the line through just above the hook. So quick were they, that one could seldom even feel a tug unless the hook got fast in their jaws. Taking off my sinker, and bending on a big hook with a wire snood, I abandoned myself to their destruction, and as fast as I hauled one alongside it was stunned, cut into three or four pieces, and thrown overboard to be devoured by its fellows. Many of the Ellice and Tokelau islanders regard these young sharks as a delicacy, as their flesh is very tender, and has not the usual unpleasant smell. In one of these young sea lawyers we found no less than five hooks, with pieces of line attached; these were duly restored to their owners.

Another two hours passed, during which we had fairly good sport, then the rain began to fall so heavily that we gave up for the day. We spent the first part of the evening in the huts, eating, smoking, and talking, and overhauling our tackle for the next day. It had been intended that about midnight we should all go crayfishing in the shallow waters along the shore of the islets, but this idea had to be abandoned in consequence of the rain having soaked the coco palms--the dead branches of which are rolled and plaited into a cylindrical form and used as torches. The method of catching crayfish is very simple: a number of men, each carrying a **kaulama** torch about 6 feet in length in the left hand, and a small scoop net in the right, walk waist-high through the water; the crayfish, dazed by the brilliant light, are whipped up into the nets and dropped into baskets carried by the women and children who follow. They can only be caught on dark, moonless nights.

*   *   *   *   *

When we returned to the village our spoils included besides a great number of fish, a few turtle and some young frigate birds. The latter were captured for the purpose of being tamed. I made many subsequent visits to the two islets, sometimes alone and sometimes with my native friends, and on each occasion I left these lovely little spots with a keen feeling of regret, for they are ideal resting-places to him who possesses a love of nature and the soul of a fisherman.

Mrs. MacLaggan's "Billy"

When Tom Denison was quite a young man he was earning a not too dishonest sort of a living as supercargo of a leaky old ketch owned by Mrs. Molly MacLaggan of Samoa, which in those days was the Land of Primeval Wickedness and Original and Imported Sin, Strong Drink, and Loose Fish generally. Captain "Bully" Hayes also lived in Samoa; his house and garden adjoined that of Mrs. MacLaggan, and at the back there was a galvanised iron cottage, inhabited by a drunken French carpenter named Leger, whose wife was a full-blooded negress, and made kava for Denison and "Bully" every evening, and used to beat Billy MacLaggan on the head with a pole about six times a day, and curse him vigorously in mongrel Martinique French. Billy MacLaggan was Mrs. Molly's male goat, and as notorious in Samoa as Bully Hayes himself.

I want to try and tell this story as clearly as possible, but there are so many people concerned, and so many things which really happened together, though each one seemed to come before the other a little and try and get into the general jumble, and every one was so confused, some fatuous people blaming the goat, and some Denison, who was generally disliked by the Germans, while Mrs. Molly said it was caused by the man with the bucket of milk, and Captain Hayes who had bribed him to do it, and nearly caused bloodshed, as the German officer who was insulted by Hayes had shot a lot of people in duels, or if he had not shot them he had stuck his sword into them in fifteen places, more or less.

Now let me explain: First of all there was Mrs. Molly, who was the hostess; then there was Hamilton, the Apia pilot and his wife; the manager of the big German firm at Matafale (he wore gold spectacles, and was very fond of Mrs. Molly, who was a widow); then there was Bully Hayes, and old Coe the American consul, and young Denison; all these were some of the local guests, and lived in Samoa, the rest were officers from a German man-of-war lying in port, and the usual respectable town loafers. Then there were Leger, the bibulous carpenter; '*Liza,* his black wife; a white policeman named Thady O'Brien, and a loafing scoundrel of a Samoan named Mataiasi, called "Matty" for brevity, who was the public flogger, and milked Mrs. MacLaggan's herd of seven imported Australian cows; and lastly the goat, and about thirty or forty of Bully Hayes's crew, and as many Samoans, who came to look at the dancing and see what they could steal, Leger and his wife and the policeman and the town flogger had charge of the refreshment tables, which for the sake of coolness had been laid out upon the wide, back verandah, and handsomely decorated with pot plants and flags from the man-of-war, and blanc-manges and jellies, and tipsy cake, and cold roast pigeons and chickens were lying around as if they weren't worth two cents.

The big wholesale store, which formed part of Mrs. Molly's house and establishment, made a fine ballroom. All the barrels of whisky and Queensland rum, and the cases of lager beer and Holland's gin, had been stowed neatly on each side, and covered over with flags and orange blossoms by Denison and Bully Hayes and his men, and the orange blossoms killed the smell of the rum so much that strangers would have thought it was sherry.

Everything went on beautifully for the first two hours, and then Mrs. Molly asked Denison to take out a very pretty young half-caste lady and get her a drink of milk. When they reached the side table where the milk should have been, they found it all gone; but O'Brien the policeman said that Mataiasi had just started off to milk another cow.

Just then Hayes came out to the refreshment tables with a lady on his arm. She was thirsty, and so "Bully" opened a large bottle of champagne, and she and he and Denison and the young half-caste lady drank it; then they drank another, and all went oft together to see Mataiasi milking the cow, which was tied up to a coconut tree just outside the fence. The cow was a yellow cow, and was standing very quietly, and just beside her Billy MacLaggan (who caused all this trouble) was lying down, working his jaws to and fro and making curious, snorting sounds in the bright and gorgeous moonlight. I forgot to say that Wm. MacLaggan was the largest and ugliest goat ever known to the memory of man, and had been taught every vice and wickedness any goat could be taught, and it is as natural for a goat to imbibe sin as it is for him to eat a cactus, or a hedgehog, or a tract.

Hayes addressed the goat by his Christian name, and asked him how he did, and Billy looked at Hayes for a second or two out of his green, sharky eyes, then he rose in a dignified manner, and came over to him to be scratched under the chin. Then he blew himself out, snorted, and rubbed his horns against the captain's knee: and Hayes remarked to Denison that the poor beggar wanted a drink, and proposed to give him a "proper one."

The goat knew perfectly well what "drink" meant, and made his vicious tail quiver; then he followed them back to the house, and stood at the foot of the steps waiting for Hayes and Tom to come out again.

On the other side of the courtyard was Mrs. MacLaggan's laundry. The door was wide open and the place was in darkness, and no one took any notice when presently Tom sauntered out of the ballroom, picked up a large plateful of tipsy-cake, and, being kind to animals, gave a piece to William, who followed him into the laundry for the rest; then Hayes came in with a quart bottle of champagne, shut the door and struck a light. Then he opened the bottle of fizz and poured it out into a deep, enamelled starching-dish, and Billy MacLaggan drank thereof, and then raised his head, with his immoral-looking beard hanging in a sodden point like a wet deck-swab, and asked for more. That is, he asked as well as any Christian and civilised goat could ask, by standing up on his hind legs like a circus-horse and making strange, unearthly noises. Then he rammed his wicked old nose into the dish again, and pushed it all round the room, trying to sop up more liquor, which wasn't there, and trod on Denison's canvas-slippered foot, and knocked over the little tin kerosene oil lamp which was standing on the floor, and when Hayes, with loud and blasphemous remarks grabbed at the ironing-blanket of the laundry-table to extinguish the flames, he pulled the table down on the top of Denison and himself and the goat and everything, for the blanket was nailed on at the four corners, and when he was down on his hands and knees, the goat being exceedingly alarmed and half-drunk, and smelling his own hair burning, put his head down and charged at the universe in general, or anything else he could hit, and he hit Hayes fair on the temple with a noise like a ship's mainmast going by the board; then the people outside burst in the door, and the creature, with a bull-like bellow, charged out among them, and landed his bony head into the stomach of Mataiasi, who was carrying the bucket of milk, and was afraid to put it down when he saw him coming; then in some way the handle of the iron bucket got on Billy MacLaggan's horns, which simply made him thirst for gore, for he thought he was being made fun of because he was in liquor. With the bucket swinging and clattering and banging around, he made a dash up on the verandah, among the pretty muslin-clad ladies and white-duck suited men, creating havoc and destruction, and smelling of kerosene and burnt hair and ancient goat, and uttering horrible, blood-curdling *bah-h-h-s*, till he got into the card-table corner, and mistaking the wide glass window for an open door, he promptly jumped through it, and fell with a shower of glass outside on to the verandah again, where Thady O'Brien and the fat German with the spectacles fell on him, and tried to hold him down, and the spectacles were ground into dust and otherwise damaged, and some of the ladies endeavouring to escape out of the hideous *melee* fell with him, and then the goat struggled to his feet with the bucket squashed flat against his forehead, and his horns covered with lace, and tulle, and bits of kid gloves, and planted one of his cloven forefeet into the shirt-front of a German officer, and smashed his watch. Then with another roar of defiance he burst through and disappeared into the wilderness at the back of Mrs. MacLaggan's garden, where he was followed by Leger, the drunken carpenter, and his wife, and nineteen Samoans, all armed with rifles. The army fired at him for two hours, and about midnight returned and reported him riddled with bullets, whereupon Mrs. Molly, who was a little hysterical at the awful mess and wreckage caused by the brute, thanked them and gave them ten dollars.

Now it so happened that Billy MacLaggan was not killed at all, for about two o'clock in the morning, as Bully Hayes and Tom Denison were sitting on the verandah of the former's house at Matautu Point, drinking brandy and soda, and dabbing arnica bandages on their various contusions, Pilot Hamilton hailed them from the front gate. He had just left the dance with his wife, and was quite sober--for Samoa. He asked them to come on with him to his place, as Billy MacLaggan, he said, was lying down in Mrs. Hamilton's kitchen, and seemed poorly, and that he hoped Hayes would forgive the poor thing, which was only a dumb animal. So Hayes and Denison went and saw William, who was now sober and looked sorry. They dressed his wounds, and Tom Denison took him on board early in the morning, intending to take him to sea till the memory of his misdeeds had toned down a bit, for Billy was a great institution in Samoa, and had many friends. Hardly a white man in the place, no matter how hard up he was, but would stand Billy a bottle of lager or a chew of tobacco. (I forgot to mention that Billy would drink anything and chew anything, except cigarettes, at which he snorted with contempt.) Now Denison's little vessel was lying quite near the German man-of-war, and was to sail next day for the Solomons if the captain was sober, and he (Denison) had a lot of work to do to get the ship ready, and whilst he was poring over accounts in the cabin about noon, a boat ran alongside and Bully Hayes came into the cabin.

"Where's Billy?" he said. "Quick, get him into my boat at once. There's a search-party coming on board, and the widow is going to give you the dirty kick-out, Tom Denison. There's been the devil to pay over that cursed goat, but I'm going to save his life all the same. But if she does sack you, you can come to me for a berth."

Billy, who was placidly eating bananas on the main deck, was at once seized and hoisted over the side into Hayes's boat, which shoved off, leaving Hayes on board to explain things to Tom.

It seemed that when the fat German manager--the man with spectacles--I mean the man who had the spectacles until Billy MacLaggan came in--the man who was courting Mrs. Molly--fell on the top of the goat, some other man trod on his face, and Leger (who was not sober enough to tell one person from another) said that he saw Tom Denison do it. Seven natives, male and female, swore that at the time alleged Tom was out on the beach bathing his crushed toe in the salt water, and using solemn British oaths; but Leger, who disliked Denison, who had once kicked him overboard violently for being drunk, not only stuck to the story, but said that Hayes and Tom had set the goat on fire on purpose to break up the dance and cause annoyance to the Germans present; also he vaguely hinted that they, Denison and Hayes, would have driven the seven cows into the ballroom but couldn't find them. Then Mrs. MacLaggan promised the fat man to sack Denison on the following morning, and at midnight, as I have said, word was brought in that Billy had been shot. But about ten in the morning Leger heard from some native that the goat was as well as ever, and on board Denison's vessel, and being a mean, spiteful little hound, off he trotted to the German manager, and said that Captain Hayes and Mr. Denison had rescued the creature. At that very moment the manager was talking to some German officers, one of whom was the man whose watch had been smashed, and as every German in Samoa hated Hayes most fervently, it was at once concluded that Hayes had trained, or suborned, or bribed, or corrupted the goat to do it. So a young lieutenant went and called upon Hayes, and demanded satisfaction for his friend, and Hayes was exceedingly rude to him, but said that if the man with the broken watch liked to meet Billy MacLaggan with his own weapons, and fight him in a goatsmanlike manner, for fifty dollars a side, he (Hayes) would put up Billy's fifty. Then the lieutenant asked for a written apology for his friend, and Hayes said that Billy couldn't write, and, anyway, he was Mrs. Molly's goat. If the man with the smashed nickel wanted an apology, why the blazes didn't he approach Mrs. MacLaggan? he asked.

Whilst Hayes was telling all this to Tom, pulling his thick beard and laughing loudly, as they paced the little vessel's deck, the search-party came on board to recover the goat. The leader bore a letter from Mrs. MacLaggan to Tom, informing him that his services as supercargo were no longer required, also that he could come ashore at once and be paid off, as his conduct was heartless, and the consuls said it might lead to serious complications, as it had been done with intent to insult the citizens of a friendly nation, one of whom, as he was aware, had made the natives cut down the price of copra half a cent. Under these circumstances, &c.

Tom grinned and showed the letter to Hayes. Then he turned to the mate.

"I've got the sack, Waters. You're in charge of this rotten, filthy old hooker now until the old man is sober."

He packed up his traps, went ashore, drew his money from Mrs. MacLaggan's cashier, and bade him goodbye.

"Where's the goat, Tom?"

"On board Bully Hayes' ship. His crool, crool mistress shall see him no more! Never more shall his plaintive call to his nannies resound o' nights among the sleeping palm-groves of the Vaisigago Valley; never----"

The cashier jumped up out of his chair and seized the dismissed supercargo by the collar.

"Stop that bosh, you rattlebrained young ass, and come and take a farewell drink."

"Never more will he butt alike the just and the unjust, the fat and bloated German merchant nor the herring-gutted Yankee skipper, nor the bare--ah--um-

-legged Samoan, nor the gorgeous consul in the solar topee. Gone is the glory of Samoa with Billy MacLaggan. Goodbye for the present, Wade, old man--I am not so proud of my new dignity--I am to be supercargo of the brig *Rona*--as to refuse to drink with you, though you are but a cashier. And give my farewell to the widow, and tell her that I bear her no ill-will, for I leave a dirty little tub of a cockroach-infested ketch for a swagger brig, where I shall wear white suits every day and feel that peace of mind which--"

"Oh, do dry up, you young beggar," said the good-natured cashier, whose laughter proved so infectious that Tom joined in.

"Come then, Wade, just another ere we part."

Now as these two were drinking in the cashier's office it happened that Thady O'Brien, the policeman (he was chief of the municipal police, and fond of drink) saw them, and invited himself to join them and also to express his sorrow at Denison's "misfortune," as he called it, for Denison was a lovable sort of youth, and often gave him drink on board. So they all sat down, Wade in the one chair, and Tom and the policeman on the table, and had several more drinks, and just then Mrs. MacLaggan came to the door, holding a note in her hand. She bowed coldly to Tom, whose three stiff drinks of brandy enabled him to give her a reproachful glance.

"Captain Hayes wants to buy one or two of the nanny-goats, to take away with him to Ponape, Mr. Wade," she said. "I shall be glad to let him have them. Please tell Leger and Mataiasi to catch them at once."

Then Mrs. MacLaggan went away, and Tom and O'Brien went down to the jetty to wait for a boat to take them on board--Tom to his duty, and O'Brien because he was thirsty again. Presently Leger and Mataiasi and a large concourse of native children came down, carrying two female goats, who, imagining they were to be cast into the sea, began to cry with great violence, and were immediately answered in a deep voice by Billy MacLaggan from over the water, whereupon Leger started to run off and tell Mrs. MacLaggan that Billy was alive, and on board the *Rona*, and Denison put out his foot and tripped him, and was at once assailed by Leger's black wife, who hit him on the head with a stick, and then herself was pushed backwards off the jetty into the water by Mr. O'Brien, taking several children and one of the goats with her, and in less than two minutes there was as pretty a fight as ever was seen. Several native police ran to help their superior officer, and a lot of dogs came with them; the dogs bit anybody and everybody indiscriminately, but most of them went for Leger and Denison, who were lying gasping together on the jetty, striving to murder each other; then a number of sailors belonging to a whaleship joined in, and tried to massacre or otherwise injure and generally maltreat the policemen, and by the time the boat from the ***Rona*** came to the rescue the jetty looked like a battlefield, and one goat was drowned, and the new supercargo was taken on board to have his excoriations attended to, for he was in a very bad state.

That is the end of the story, which I have told in a confused sort of away, I admit, because there are so many things in it, though I could tell a lot more about the adventures of Billy MacLaggan, after he went to sea with Captain Bully Hayes.

An Island Memory

CHAPTER I

From early dawn wild excitement had prevailed in the great native village on the shores of Port Lele, and on board two ships which were anchored on the placid waters of the land-locked harbour. As the fleecy, cloud-like mist which, during the night, had enveloped the forest-clad spurs and summit of Mont Buache, was dispelled by the first airs of the awakened trade wind and the yellow shafts of sunrise, a fleet or canoes crowded with natives put off from the sandy beach in front of the king's house, and paddled swiftly over towards the ships, the captains of which only awaited their arrival to weigh and tow out through the passage.

As the mist lifted, Cayse, the master of the *Iroquois* of Sagharbour, stepped briskly up on the poop, and hailed the skipper of the other vessel, a small, yellow-painted barque of less than two hundred tons.

"Are you ready, Captain Ross?"

"All ready," was the answer; "only waiting for the military," and then followed a hoarse laugh.

Cayse, a little, grizzled, and leathern-faced man of fifty, replied by an angry snarl, then turned to his mate, who stood beside him awaiting his orders.

"Get these natives settled down as quickly as possible, Mr. North, then start to heave-up and loose sails. I reckon we'll tow out in an hour. The king will be here presently in his own boat. Hoist it aboard."

North nodded in silence, and was just moving on to the main deck, when Cayse stopped him.

"You don't seem too ragin' pleased this mornin', Mr. North, over this business. Naow, as I told you yesterday, I admire your feelin's on the subject, but I can't afford--"

The mate's eyes blazed with anger.

"And I tell you again that I won't have anything to do with it. I know my duty, and mean to stick to it. I shipped for a whaling voyage, and not to help savages to fight. Take my advice and give it up. Money got in this way will do you no good."

Cayse shifted his feet uneasily.

"I can't afford to sling away the chance of earnin' two or three thousan' dollars so easy. An' you'll hev to do your duty to me. Naow, look here--"

North raised his hand.

"That will do. I have said I will do my duty as mate, but not a hand's turn will I take in such bloody work as you and the skipper of that crowd of Sydney cutthroats and convicts are going into for the sake of six thousand dollars."

"Well, I reckon we can do without you. Any one would think we was going piratin', instead of helping the king of this island to his rights. Naow, just tell me--"

Again the mate interrupted him.

"I am going for'ard to get the anchor up, and will obey all your orders as far as the working of the ship is concerned--nothing more."

An hour later the two vessels, their decks crowded with three hundred savages, armed with muskets, spears, and clubs, were towed out through the narrow, reef-bound passage, and with the now freshening trade wind filling their sails, set a course along the coast which before sunset would bring them to Leasse, on the lee side of the island. But presently, in response to a signal from the *Lucy May*, the whaler lay to; a boat put off from the smaller ship, and Captain Ross came alongside, clambered over the bulwarks and joined Cayse and the young king of Port Lele, who were awaiting him on the poop, to discuss with him the plan of surprise and slaughter of the offending people of Leasse.

*   *   *   *   *

Nearly a week before the *Iroquois* had run into Port Lele to refresh before pro-ceeding westward and northward to the Bonin Islands in pursuance of her cruise. Charlik, the king, was delighted to see Cayse, for in the days when his father was king the American captain had conveyed a party of one hundred Strong's Island-ers from Port Lele to MacAskill's Island, landed them in his boats during the night, and stood off and on till daylight, when they returned reeking from their work of slaughter upon the sleeping people, and bringing with them some scores of women and children as captives. For this service the king had given Cayse half a ton of turtle-shell, and the services of ten young men as seamen for as long a time as the *Iroquois* cruised in the Pacific on that voyage. When Charlik's father was dy-ing, he called his head chiefs around him, and gave the boy into their care with these words--"Here die I upon my mat like a woman, long before my time, and to-morrow my spirit will hear the mocking laughs of the men of Mout and Leasse, when they say, 'Sikra is dead; Sikra was but an empty boaster.'"

Then his son spoke.

"Not many days shall they laugh. They shall be destroyed all, all, all of them."

The king touched his son's hand.

"Those are good words. But be not too hasty. Wait till the American comes again. He will help with his men and guns. But he is a greedy man. Yet spare noth-ing; give him all the silver and gold money I have stored by for his return, and all the turtle-shell that can be gathered together. And let there be not even one little child left in Mout or Leasse."

Charlik was a lad or seventeen when his savage old father died, and for a year after his death he harried and distressed his people by his exactions. All day long the men toiled at making coconut oil, and at night time they watched along the beaches for the hawk-bill turtle; the oil they put into huge butts, which stood in the king's boat-sheds, and the costly turtle-shell was taken by the young ruler and locked up in the seamen's chests which lined the inside wall of the great council-house. And no man durst now fire a musket at a wild pig, for powder and ball had been made *tapu*--such things were given up to the chiefs, lest they might be wasted, and every morning three young men climbed up the rugged side of Mont Buache, to keep a look-out for the ship whose captain would help their master to wreak a bloody vengeance upon the rebellious people of Leasse.

At the end of the sixteenth month of watching, a sail appeared coming from the southward, and the watchers on the mountain-top sped down to the king's house, and sinking upon their knees in the courtyard of coral slabs, whispered their news to one of the king's serving-men, who, with a musket in his hand and a cutlass girt around his naked waist, stood sentry before the youthful despot's sleeping-room.

"Good," said the king to Kanka, his head chief; "'tis surely the American Kesa,[13] for this is the month in which he said he would return. Let the women make ready a great feast, and launch my three boats, so that if the wind fail, when the sun is high, they may help to drag the ship into Lele."

Then came the sound of beating drums, and the long, mournful note of the conch-shells calling the wild people together to prepare for the ship. Turtle were lifted from their walled-in prison holes on the reef, hogs were strangled, and the king's wives went hither and thither among his slave women, bidding them hasten to kindle the ovens, whilst children went out into the great canework cage, wherein were hundreds of the king's wild pigeons, and seizing the birds, began to pluck them alive.

An hour passed. Charlik, sitting in a European chair, was watching the wild bustle and excitement around him in the courtyard, when his eye fell on the three messengers, who, with bent head and bended knees, were awaiting his further commands.

Beckoning to a young, light-skinned woman, who stood near him, he bade her bring him three of his best pearl-shell bonito hooks. They were brought, and taking them from her, he threw them to the men.

"Ye have watched well," he said. "There is thy reward. Now go and eat and sleep."

With eyes sparkling with pleasure, the young men each took up his precious gift, and with crouching forms crept slowly over to the further side of the courtyard, where they were waited upon by women with food.

Presently the fair young woman--his sister Se--returned to her brother's side.

"The ship is near," she said, and then her voice faltered; "but it is not the ship of

Kesa. It is but a small ship, and she hath but two boats. Kesa's had five."

"What lies are these?" said the young savage fiercely. "Go look again."

The girl left him, to return a few minutes later with grey-headed old Kanka, who in response to an inquiring look from his master, bent his head and said slowly--

"'Tis a strange ship--one that never before have we seen in Lele."

The youth made him no answer. He merely raised his arm and pointed his finger at the three messengers.

"Then they have lied to me. Bring them here to me."

Kanka stepped over to where the fated men were sitting. They rose at his behest, and crept over to the king; behind them, at some invisible sign given by him, followed a man with a heavy club of **toa** wood. The clamour which had filled the courtyard ceased, and terrified silence fell. One by one the messengers knelt upon the coral flags--no need for them to ask for mercy from Charlik, the savage son of a bloodstained father. The bearer of the club held the weapon knob downward, and watched the king's face for the signal of death. He nodded, and then, one after another of the men were struck and fell prone upon the stones. With scowling eyes Charlik regarded them for a moment or two in silence, then he turned unconcernedly away, as some of his slaves came forward and carried the bodies out of sight.

Suddenly he sprang to his feet, as a loud, long cry, first from a single throat, and then echoed and reechoed by a hundred more, came upward from the beach.

"A ship! A ship! Another ship! The ship of Kesa!"

Bidding his sister and the old chief Kanka to come with him, Charlik quickly left the house, and walking through a grove of breadfruit trees, reached a spot from where he had a full view of the open sea. There right in the passage was a small barque; and, almost within hail, and just rounding the northern horn of the reef was a larger vessel, one glance at which told Charlik that it was the American whaler for which he had so long waited. In less than an hour they were at anchor abreast of the king's house, and the two captains were being rowed ashore. They met on the beach. The master of the smaller vessel was a tall, broad-shouldered man, armed with a pair of pistols and a cutlass. Striding over the sand he held out his hand to the American.

"Good day. My name's Ross, barque *Lucy May*, of Sydney, from the New Hebrides to Hong Kong with sandalwood."

"Glad to meet ye. My name is Cayse, ship *Iroquois*, bound on a sperm whalin' cruise."

Further speech was denied them, for suddenly the thronging and excited natives around them drew aside right and left as Charlik, with a face beaming with smiles, came up to Cayse with outstretched hand, and greeted him warmly in English. Then he turned quickly to the Englishman and shook hands with him also, and asked him from whence he came.

"From Sydney. I came here to get wood, water, and provisions."

"Good. You can get all you want. Have you muskets and bullets to sell?"

"I can spare you some."

"Ah, that is good. I want plenty, plenty. Now come to my house and eat and drink; then we can talk."

It was well on towards sunset before Charlik and Cayse had finished their talk. Ross meanwhile had gone on board the barque for some firearms which he was giving the king in exchange for several boatloads of provisions. When he returned, with two of his crew carrying six muskets, a keg of powder, and a bag of bullets, Cayse met him on the threshold of the king's house.

"Come inside, mister. The king wants to talk to you on a matter of business. I reckon you an' me together can do what he wants done. But jest come along with me first. I want to show you the kind of fellow he is when he gets upset."

The master of the sandalwooder followed the American across the wide courtyard to some native houses. Stopping in front of one, from which the low murmur of women's voices, broken now and then by a wailing cry, proceeded, he desired Ross to look in through the doorway. A small fire of coconut shells was burning in the centre of the room, and *by* its light Ross saw several women crouched round the bodies of three men, performing the last offices for the dead. They looked at the white strangers with apathetic indifference, but ceased their labours whilst Ross bent down and examined the still faces. His scrutiny was brief, but it was enough.

Cayse gave a sniggering laugh. "I reckon you'll feel sorter startled, mister, when I tell you that you were the cause of those men getting clubbed, hey?"

Ross frowned angrily. "What are you driving at? What the devil had I to do with it?"

"On'y this. You see I'm the white-headed boy with this young island cock, an' he's been expectin' to see the *Iroquois* for quite a time. Your barque happened to heave in sight first, an' these three fellows who were standin' mast-head watch up thar on the mountain, came tearin' down an' reported that it was my old hooker. Charlik bein' a most impatient young fellow, had 'em clubbed on the spot; he should hev waited another five minutes. Come on, he's ready to talk business with us now."

In the centre of the big council room Charlik, attended by his sister, was seated upon a mat. A couple of brightly burning ship's lanterns suspended from the beams overhead, revealed the figures of a score of armed natives, seated with their backs to the canework walls of the room; midway between them and the young king were two seamen's chests, beside which crouched the half-naked, tatooed form or old Kanka.

Followed by the sailors carrying the muskets, the two captains walked over the soft, springy floor of mats, and seated themselves facing the young man. His eye lit up at the sight of the arms, and then he desired Ross to tell his men to withdraw. Then as the sound of their footsteps died away, he looked at Cayse and said briefly--

"Go on, capen. You talk."

Cayse went into the subject at once.

"Captain Ross, do you want to earn three thousand dollars?"

"Don't mind."

"Neither do I. Well, just listen. The king here has three thousand dollars in cash and three thousand dollars' worth of coconut ile and turtle-shell. Now, if you and I will help him to do a bit of fightin' it's ours. The money and shell is here in this room, the ile is in the sheds near by. If you agree, the king will hand us over the money now, and we can ship the ile in the morning."

Ross thought a moment, then he said suspiciously--

"Why are you giving me a chance?"

"Not from any feelin' of affection for you, mister," answered Cayse with his peculiar snarl, "but because I ain't able to do the whole business myself--if I could I wouldn't ask *you* to come in. Now, I noticed this mornin' that you carry a big crew, and have six guns, and I reckon thet you hev to use 'em sometimes in your business?"

Ross laughed grimly. "All of us sandalwooding ships carry a few nine-pounders as well as plenty of small arms. We are allowed to do so by the Governor of New South Wales."

"Just so. Well, now, listen. This island is governed by two chiefs; this one here, Charlik, has most people, but the other lot, who live on the lee side of the island, rebelled against his father more'n ten years ago. They've had a good many fights, an' in the last one these Lele people got badly whipped. Charlik is the proper king, but ever since a white man named Ledyard went to live with the Leasse people, they've refused to pay tribute. This Ledyard is the cause of all the trouble, and he has taught his natives how to fight European fashion. There's only about six hundred of 'em altogether--men, women, and children--eh, Charlik?"

The young chief nodded in assent.

"Now, by a bit of luck, news came up the other day by one of Charlik's spies that Ledyard has gone away to Ponape in a cutter he has built. It will take him two or three weeks to go there and back, and now is the time for Charlik to wipe out old scores--the Leasse people won't stand much of a chance agin' a night attack by three hundred of Charlik's people. If Ledyard was there it would be different."

Ross soon made his decision. He was a man utterly without pity, and Cayse who, while inciting others to slaughter for the sake of his own gain, yet had some grains of compunction in his nature, almost shuddered when the master of the *Lucy May* laughed hoarsely and said--

"It's a bargain--just the thing that my crowd could tackle and carry through themselves. Two voyages ago me and my beauties wiped out every living soul on one of the Cartaret's Islands. I'll tell you the yarn some day. But look here, king, can't we make another deal about the women and children. Let me keep as many of them as I have room for aboard, and I'll pay for them in muskets and powder and bullets."

"What do you want with them?"

"Sell them to old Abba Dul, the king of the Pelews. I've done business with him before."

Charlik called Kanka over to him, and the two spoke in low tones. Then the young ruler of Lele shook his head.

"No. There must be but one left to live--the white man's wife. Now we shall count this money."

The boxes were carried over directly under the rays of the lamps and opened, the bags containing the money lifted out, the coins counted, and then evenly divided between the two wolves.

On the following morning the casks of oil were rolled down to the beach and rafted off to the two ships, and before dawn, on the fourth day, Ross and his fellow-ruffian sent word ashore to the king that all was ready, and that he and his fighting men could come on board at once and proceed on their dreadful mission.

CHAPTER II

As the two captains and their ferocious young employer sat on the snow-white poop of the *Iroquois* and discussed the plan of attack, the ship and barque kept closely together, so closely that North, who had not yet placed foot on board the sandalwooder, had now an opportunity of looking down upon her decks, and watching the actions of those who manned her. A more ragged and desperate looking lot of ruffians he had never seen in his life; and their wild, unkempt appearance was in perfect accord with the *Lucy May* herself, whose dirty, yellow sides were stained from stem to stern with long streaks and broad patches of iron-rust. Aloft she was in as equally a bad condition, and North and his fellow-officers, used to the trimness and unceasing care of a whaleship's sails and running gear, looked with contempt at the disorder and neglect everywhere visible. On deck, however, some attempt at setting things ship-shape were being made by the two mates and boatswain, the six guns were being overhauled, and a pile of muskets lying on the main hatch were being examined and passed up to the poop one by one, to old Kanka, who was in command of the contingent of Lele natives on board the barque. Similar preparations with small arms were being made on board the *Iroquois* by her crew which, largely composed of Chilenos, Portuguese, and Polynesians, had eagerly accepted the offer of twenty dollars for each man for a few hours' fighting. North alone had spoken against and tried to dissuade his fellow-officers from taking any active part in the expedition, but his remonstrances fell upon unheeding ears. The details of the scheme to surprise the unsuspecting inhabitants of the two villages had filled him with unutterable horror and indignation, and all sorts of wild plans formed in his brain to prevent the accomplishment of the cruel deed. For the consequences of such interference to himself he cared nothing. He was alone in the world, and had no thought beyond that of making enough money to enable him to one day buy a ship of his own. Once, as he passed the trio on the poop, and glanced at the smooth, olive-coloured features of the young king, who, with anticipative zest, was fondling a rifle which Ross had brought on board for him, he felt inclined to whip a belaying-pin out of the rail and bring it crashing down upon his skull. Had there been any other ship but the *Lucy May* near, he would have left the *Iroquois* that moment. But help was coming to his troubled mind.

An hour before sunset the two vessels ran into a little harbour, then called Port Lottin, but now known as South Harbour by the few wandering whalers which sometimes touch at the island. Here, ere it became dark, the natives, with fourteen of the *Lucy May's* crew under Ross, were landed. They were to march at early morning, cross the mountain range which intervened between South Harbour and Leasse, and then, hidden by the dense forest, await the appearance of the ships off the doomed villages on the following afternoon. The six boats--two from the *Lucy May* and four from the *Iroquois*--were to pull ashore as soon as the ships were off Leasse and take up positions, three to the north and three to the south, so as to cut off all who attempted to escape along the beaches from the attack which would be made by Ross. Charlik was to command one of the boat parties, Cayse the other, and should any canoes with fugitives attempt to gain the open sea, they were to be sunk by the *Lucy May's* guns, for she was to anchor in such a position that an escaping canoe would have to pass within fifty yards of her.

*   *   *   *   *

Eight bells had struck, and North, who had declined to join the captain and his fellow-officers at supper, was sitting in his cabin smoking and listening to the soft hum of the surf on the barrier reef a mile away. On deck all was quiet, only the fourth mate and three of the hands were keeping watch, the rest of the crew who were not turned in had gone ashore to witness a dance given by King Charlik's warriors.

Suddenly he heard a footfall on the cabin deck, and then some one said in a low voice--

"May I come in, sir?"

North, recognising the voice as that of a young man named Macy, his own harpooner, at once bade him enter.

Macy, a sunburnt, blue-eyed youth, closed the cabin door behind him, and held up his finger to enjoin silence.

"I've only just now heard, sir, that you will not take a hand in this work which is going on. Neither will I, sir; for those damned savages are going to kill all the poor women and children. I've come to ask you what I'm to do if I'm ordered away in the boat? My God! Mr. North, must we all be turned into a gang of murderers like those fellows on the *Lucy May!*"

The officer shook the young seaman's hand. "I for one will have no hand in it, my lad; and I wish there were more of us on board of our way of thinking. I wish we could leave the ship. I would rather die of thirst on the open ocean ... Macy, my lad, will you stand to me?"

"Stand to you, sir! Aye, Mr. North. If you mean to take to our boat, sir, I am with you."

"No," answered North in a whisper. "That, after all, would only save us two from being mixed up in this murderous business--I want to prevent it altogether. Have you heard how far it is across the island to this place Leasse?"

"Seven miles, sir, over the mountains."

"And twenty by the boats! Macy, I am determined to leave the ship to-night, cut across the island, and save the poor people from massacre. Will you come? We may pay for it with our lives."

The harpooner raised his rough hand. "We must all die some day, sir."

For some minutes they conversed in whispered tones; then Macy slipped on deck, and North took his pistols from their racks, filled his coat pockets with ammunition, and then followed him. His own boat was lying astern.

Telling the cooper, who was the only one of the afterguard on deck, that he was going ashore to look at the dance, and that only Macy and another hand need come with him, North ordered the boat to be hauled alongside. A quarter of an hour later he and Macy stepped out upon the shore under the shadow of a high bluff, and quite out of view from Ross and his party, although the many camp-fires cast long lines of light across the sleeping waters of the little harbour.

Informing the boat-keeper that they should return in a couple of hours, the two men first walked along the beach in the direction of the encampment. Then once out of sight from the boat, they struck inland into a deep valley through which, Macy said, a narrow track led up to the range, and then downwards to the two villages. After a careful search the track was found, and the bright stars shining through the canopy of leaves overhead gave them sufficient light to pursue their way. For two hours they toiled along through the silent forest, hearing no sound except now and then the affrighted rush of some startled wild boar, and, far distant, the dull cry of the ever-restless breakers upon the coral reef. At last the summit of the range was reached, and they sat down to rest upon the thick carpet of fallen leaves which covered the ground. Here North took a spirit-flask from his jacket, and Macy and he drank in turns.

"Do you know, sir," said Macy, as he returned the flask to the officer, "that there's a white man living at this village?"

"He's not there now, Macy. He's gone away to another island in his cutter."

"I know that, sir. I've heard all about it from one of the chaps on the *Lucy May*. The man's name is Ledyard, and this young devil's-limb of a king hates him like poison--for two reasons. One is, that Ledyard, who settled in Leasse a few years ago, taught the people there how to use their muskets in a fight, when Charlik's father tried to destroy them time and again; the other is that his wife is a white woman--or almost a white woman, a Bonin Island Portuguese--and Charlik means to get her. When Ledyard comes back in his cutter he will walk into a trap, and be killed as soon as he steps ashore."

North struck his hand upon the ground. "And to think that I have sailed with such a villain as Cayse, who--"

"That's not all. Ledyard has two children. Charlik has given orders for them to be killed, as he says he only wants the woman! Ross, I believe, wanted him to spare 'em, but the young cut-throat said 'No.' I heard all this from two men--the chap from the *Lucy May* and one of Charlik's fighting men, who speaks English and seems to have a soft place in his heart for Ledyard."

The mate of the *Iroquois* sprang to his feet. "The cold-blooded wretches! Come on, Macy. We **must** get there in time."

For another two hours they made steady progress through the darkened forest aisles, and then as they emerged out upon a piece of open country, they saw far beneath them the gleaming sea. And here, amidst a dense patch of pandanus palms, the path they had followed came to an end. Pushing their way through the thorny leaves, which tore the skin from their hands and faces, Macy exclaimed excitedly--

"We're all right, sir. I can see a light down there. It must be a fire on the beach."

Heedless of the unknown dangers of the deep descent, and every now and then tripping and falling over the roots of trees and fallen timber, they again came out into the open, and there, two hundred feet below them, they saw the high-peaked, saddle-backed houses of Leasse village standing clearly out in the starlight. But at this point their further progress was barred by a cliff, which seemed to extend for half a mile on both sides of them. Cautiously feeling their way along its ledge they sought in vain for a path.

"We must hail them, Macy. There will be sure to be plenty of them who can speak a little English and show us the way to get down."

Returning as quickly as possible to the spot immediately over the village, the officer gave a long, loud hail.

"***Below there, you sleepers!***"

The hoarse, shrieking notes of countless thousands of roosting sea-birds, as they rose in alarm from their perches in the forest trees, mingled with the barking of dogs from the village, and then came a wild cry of alarm from a human throat.

Waiting for a few moments till the clamour had somewhat subsided, the two men again hailed in unison.

"***Below there! Awake, you sleepers!***"

Another furious outburst of yelping and barking--through which ran the quavering of voices of the affrighted natives--smote the stillness of the night. Then the bright light of torches of coconut leaves flashed below, nude figures ran swiftly to and fro among the houses, and then came a deep-voiced answering hail in English--

"***Hallo there! Who hails***?"

"Two white men," was the officer's quick reply. "We cannot get down. Bear a hand with a torch; we have lost the track." Then as something flashed across his mind, he added, "Who are you? Are you a white man?"

"Yes. I am Tom Ledyard."

"Thank God for that! Send a light quickly. You and your people are in deadly danger."

In a few minutes the waiting men saw the gleam of torches amid the trees to their right, and presently a tall, bearded, white man appeared, followed by half a dozen natives. All were armed with muskets, whose barrels glinted and shone in the firelight.

Springing forward to meet him, North told his story in as few words as possible.

Ledyard's dark face paled with passion. "By heaven, they shall get a bloody welcome! Now, come, sir; follow me. You must need rest badly."

As they passed through the village square, now lit up by many fires and filled with alarmed natives, Ledyard called out in his deep tones--

"Gather ye together, my friends. The son of the Slaughterer is near. Send a man fleet of foot to Mout and bid him tell Nena, the chief, and his head men to come to my house quickly, else in a little while our bones will be gnawed by Charlik's dogs."

Then with North and Macy besides him, he entered his house, the largest in the village. A woman, young, slender, and fair-skinned, met them at the door. Behind her were some terrified native women, one of whom carried Ledyard's youngest child in her arms.

"'Rita, my girl," said Ledyard, placing his hand on his wife's shoulder and speaking in English, "these are friends. They have come to warn us. That young hell-pup, Charlik, is attacking us tomorrow. But quick, girl, get something for these gentlemen to eat and drink."

But North and the harpooner were too excited to eat, and, seated opposite their host, they listened eagerly to him as he told them of his plans to repel the attack; of the bitter hatred that for ten years had existed between the people of Leasse and the old king; and then--he set his teeth--how that Se, the friendly sister of the young king, had once sent a secret messenger to him telling him to guard his wife well, for her brother had made a boast that when Leasse and Mout were given to the flames only Cerita should be spared.

"Then, ten days ago, Mr. North, thinking that this young tiger-cub Charlik knew that these people here were well prepared to resist an attack, I left in my cutter on a trading voyage to Ponape. Three days out the vessel began to make water so badly that I had to beat back. I only came ashore yesterday."

He rose and walked to and fro, muttering to himself. Then he spoke again.

"Mr. North, and you, my friend"--turning to Macy--"have saved me and those I love from a sudden and cruel death. What can I do to show my gratitude? You cannot now return to your ship; will you join your fortunes with mine? I have long thought of leaving this island and settling in Ponape. There is money to be made there. Join me and be my partners. My cutter is now hauled up on the beach--if she were fit to go to sea we could leave the island to-night. But that cannot be done. It will take me a week to put her in proper repair--and to-morrow we must fight for our lives."

North stretched out his hand. "Macy and I will stand by you, Ledyard. We do not want to ever put foot again on the deck of the *Iroquois*."

CHAPTER III

The story of that day of bloodshed and horror, when Charlik and his white allies sought to exterminate the whole community, cannot here be told in *all* its dreadful details. Seventy years have come and gone since then, and there are but two or three men now living on the island who can speak of it with knowledge as a tale of "the olden days when we were heathens." Let the rest of the tale be told in the words of one of those natives of Leasse, who, then a boy, fought side by side with Ledyard, North, and Macy.

*   *   *   *   *

"The sun was going westward in the sky when the two ships rounded the point and anchored in what you white men now call Coquille Harbour. We of Leasse, who watched from the shore, saw six boats put off, filled with men. There pulled inside the reef, and went to the right towards Mout; three went to the left. Letya (Ledyard), with the two white strangers who had come to him in the night, and two hundred of our men, had long before gone into the mountains to await Charlik and his fighting men, and their white friends. They--Letya and the Leasse people-

-made a trap for Charlik's men in the forest. Charlik himself was in the boats with the other white men. He wanted to see the people of Leasse and Mout driven into the water, so that he might shoot at them with a new rifle which Kesa or the other ship captain--I forget which--had given to him. But he wanted most of all to get Cerita, the wife of Letya, the white man. Only Cerita was to live. These were Charlik's words. He did not know that her husband had returned from the sea. Had he known that, he would not have given all his money and all his oil to the two white captains to help him to make Leasse and Mout desolate and give our bones to his dogs to eat.

"It was a great trap--the trap prepared by Letya; and Charlik's men and the white men with them fell in it. They fell as a stone falls in a deep well, and sinks and is no more seen of men.

"This was the manner of the trap: The path down the cliff was between two high walls of rock; at the foot of the cliff was a thick clump of high pandanus trees growing closely together. In between these trees Letya built a high barrier of logs, encompassing the outlet of the path to Leasse. This barrier was a half circle; the two ends touched the edge of the cliff, and the centre was hidden among the pandanus trees. On the top of this barrier the men of Leasse waited with loaded muskets; lower down on the ground were others, they too had loaded muskets. On the top of the cliff where the path led down, fifty men were hidden. They were hidden in the thick scrub which we call *oap*. *Oap* is a good thing in which to hide from an enemy, and then spring from and slay him suddenly.

"I, who was then a boy, saw all this. I heard Letya, our white man, tell the head of our village that Charlik's men would enter into the trap and perish. Then kava was made, and Letya and the head men drank. Kava is good, but rum is better to make men fight. We had no rum, but we had great love for Letya and his wife, and his two children, and great hate for Charlik. So we said, 'If this is death, it is death,' and every man went to his post--some to the barrier at the foot of the cliff, and some to the thicket of *oap* on the summit. Cerita, the wife of Letya the Englishman, was weeping. She was weeping because Nena, the chief of Mout, was waiting in the house to kill her if her husband should be slain. But she did not weep because of the fear of death; it was for her children she wept. That is the way of women. What is the life of a child to the life of a man?

"Nena was my father's brother. He was a brave man, but was too old to fight, for his eyes were dimmed by many years. So he sat beside Cerita and her two children, with a long knife in his hand and waited. He covered his face with a mat and waited. It was right for him to do this, for Letya was a great man; and his wife, although she was a foreigner, was an honoured woman. Therefore though Nena might not look upon her face at other times, he could kill her if Letya said she must die. This was quite right and correct. A wife must be guided by her husband and do what is right and correct, and avoid scandal.

"For many hours the women in the houses waited in silence. Then suddenly they heard the thunder of two hundred guns, and the roaring of voices, then more muskets. They ran out of the houses and looked up to the cliff, and lo! the sky was bright as day, for when Charlik's people and the white men walked into the trap in the darkness, Letya and our people set alight great heaps of dry leaves and scrub, which were placed all along the barrier of logs. This was done so that they could see better to shoot. There were thirty or forty of Charlik's men killed by that volley. The white man who was leading them was very brave; he tried to climb over the barrier, but fell back dead, for a man named Sru thrust a whale-lance into his heart. All this time the other white men and the rest of Charlik's people were firing their muskets, but their bullets only hit the heavy logs of the barrier, and Letya and our people killed them very easily by putting their muskets through the spaces. When the sailors saw their captain fall, they tried to run away, and the Lele warriors ran with them. But when they reached the path which led up between the cliff, it too was blocked, and many of them became jammed together between the walls, and these were all killed very easily--some with bullets, and some with big stones. Then those that were left ran round and found inside the trap, trying to get out. They were like rats in a cask, and our people kept killing them as they ran. Some of them--about thirty--did climb over, but all were killed, for when they jumped down on the other side our people were there waiting. At last four of the sailors made a big hole by tearing out two posts, and rushed out, followed by the Lele men. Letya was the first man to meet the sailors, and he told them to surrender. Two of them threw down their arms, but the other two ran at Letya, and one of them ran his cutlass into him. It went in at the stomach, and Letya fell. We killed all these white sailors, but some of the Lele men escaped. That was a great pity, but then how can these things be helped?" The two strange white men who were fighting beside Le|tya, picked him up, and they carried him into his house. He was not dead, but he said, 'I shall soon die, take me to my wife.' I did not go with them to the house. I went into the barrier with the other youths to kill the wounded. It is a foolish thing not to kill wounded men; they may get better and kill you. So we killed them. There were fourteen white men slain in that fight beside their captain.

"Before it was daylight some of our men set out along the beach to look for the boats. They did not want to kill any more white men, but they did want to kill Charlik. They were very fortunate, for before they had gone far on their way they saw three of the boats coming along close in to the beach. So they hid behind some rocks. Charlik was in the first boat; he was standing in the bow pointing out the way. When he came very close they all fired together, and Charlik's life was gone. He fell dead into the sea. Then the boats all turned seaward, and pulled hard for the ships. Then before long, we saw the other three boats going back to the ships; in these last were four of Charlik's men who had escaped. The boats were quickly pulled up, and the ships sailed away, for those on board were terrified when they heard that all the white men they had sent to fight were dead.

"Letya did not die at once--not for two days. Cerita his wife and two white men watched beside him all this time. Before he died he called the head men to him, and said that he gave his small ship to the two white men, together with many other things. All his money he gave to his wife, and told her she must go away with the white men, who would take her back to her own people. To the head men he gave many valuable things, such as tierces of tobacco and barrels of powder. This was quite right and proper, and showed he knew what was correct to do before he died. We buried him on the little islet over there called Besi.

"The two white men and Cerita and her two children went away in the little ship. But they did not go to Cerita's country: they remained at Ponape, and there the tall man of the two--the officer--married Cerita. All this we learnt a year afterwards from the captain of a whaling ship. It was quite right and proper for Letya's widow to marry so quickly, and to marry the man who had been a friend to her husband."

A Hundred Fathoms Deep

There is still a world or discovery open to the ichthyologist who, in addition to scientific knowledge, is a lover of deep-sea fishing, has some nerve, and is content to undergo some occasional rough experiences, if he elects to begin his researches among the many island groups of the North and South Pacific. I possessed, to some extent, the two latter qualifications; the former, much to my present and lasting regret, I did not. Nearly twenty-six years ago the vessel in which I sailed as supercargo was wrecked on Strong's Island, the eastern outlier of the fertile Caroline Archipelago, and for more than twelve months I devoted the greater part of my time to traversing the mountainous island from end to end, or, accompanied by a hardy and intelligent native, in fishing, either in the peculiarly-formed lagoon at the south end, or two miles or so outside the barrier reef.

The master of the vessel, I may mention, was the notorious, over maligned, and genial Captain Bully Hayes, and from him I had learnt a little about some of the generally unknown deep-sea fish of Polynesia and Melanesia. He had told me that when once sailing between Aneityum and Tanna, in the New Hebrides, shortly after a severe volcanic eruption on the former island had been followed by a submarine convulsion, his brig passed through many hundreds of dead and dying fish of great size, some of which were of a character utterly unknown to any of his native crew--men who came from all parts of the North and South Pacific. More remarkable still, some of these fish had never before been seen by the inhabitants of the islands near which they were found. There were, he said, some five or six kinds, but they were all of the groper family. One of three which was brought on board was discovered floating on the surface when the ship was five miles off Tanna. A boat was lowered, but on getting up to it, the crew found they were unable to lift it from the water; it was, however, towed to the ship, hoisted on board, and cut into three parts, the whole of which were weighed, and reached over 300 lbs. In colour it was a dull grey, with large, closely-adhering scales about the size of a florin; the fins, tail, and lips were blue. Another one, weighing less, had a differently-shaped head, with a curious, pipe-like mouth; this was a uniform dull blue. A similar upturning from the ocean's dark depths of strange fish occurred during a submarine earthquake near Rose Island, a barren spot to the south-west of Samoa. The disturbance threw up vast numbers of fish upon the reefs of Manua, the nearest island of the group, and the natives looked upon their great size and peculiar appearance with unbounded astonishment.

Without desiring to bore the reader with unnecessary details of my own experiences in the South Seas, but because the statement bears on the subject of this article--a subject which has been my delight since I was a boy of ten years of age--I may say that, nine years after the loss of Captain Hayes's vessel on Strong's Island, I was again shipwrecked on Peru, one of the Gilbert, or, as we traders call them, the "Line" Islands. Here I was so fortunate as to take up my residence with one of the local traders, a Swiss named Frank Voliero, who was an ardent deep-sea fisherman, and whose catches were the envy and wonder of the wild and intractable natives among whom he lived; for he had excellent tackle, which enabled him to fish at depths seldom tried by the natives, who have no reason to go beyond sixty or eighty fathoms. In the long interval that had elapsed since my fishing days in the Carolines and my arrival at Peru Island, I had gained such experience in my hobby in many other parts of the Pacific as falls to few men, and the desire to fish in deep water, and get something that astonished the natives of the various islands, had become a passion with me. Voliero and myself went out together frequently, and, did space permit, I should like to describe the fortune that attended us at Peru, as well as my fishing adventures at Strong's Island.

In a former work I have endeavoured to describe that extraordinary nocturnal-feeding fish, the *palu*, and the manner of its capture by the Malayo-Polynesian islanders of the Equatorial Pacific, and in the present article I shall try to convey to my readers an idea of deep-sea fishing in the South Seas generally. When I was living on the little island of Nanomaga (one of the Ellice Group, situated about 600 miles to the north-west of Samoa), as the one resident trader, I found myself in--if I may use the term--a marine paradise, as far as fishing went. The natives were one and all expert fishermen, extremely jealous of their reputation of being not only the best and most skilful men in Polynesia in the handling of their frail canoes in a heavy surf, but also of being deep-learned in the lore of deep-sea fishing.

My arrival at the island caused no little commotion among the young bloods, each of whose chances of gaining the girl of his heart, and being united to her by the local Samoan missionary teacher, depended in a great measure upon his ability to provide sustenance for her from the sea; for Nanomaga, like the rest of the Ellice Group, is but little more than a richly-verdured sandbank, based upon a foundation of coral, and yielding nothing to its people but coconuts and a coarse species of taro, called puraka. The inhabitants, in their low-lying atolls, possess no running streams, no fertile soil, in which, as in the mountainous isles of Polynesia, the breadfruit, the yam, and the sweet potato grow and flourish side by side with such rich and luscious fruits as the orange and banana, and pineapple--they have but the beneficent coconut and the evergiving sea to supply their needs. And the sea is kind to them, as Nature meant it to be to her own children.

The native missionary at Nanomaga was a Samoan. He was intended by nature to be a warrior, a leader of men; or--and no higher praise can I give to his dauntless courage--a boat-header on a sperm whaler. Strong of arm and quick of eye, he was the very man to either throw the harpoon or deal the death-giving thrust or the lance to the monarch of the ocean world; but fate or circumstance had made him a missionary instead. He was a fairly good missionary, but a better fisherman.

Three miles from Nanomaga is a submerged reef, marked on the chart as the Grand Coral Reef, but known to the natives as Tia Kau, "the reef." It is in reality a vast mountain of coral, whose bases lie two hundred fathoms deep, with a flattened summit of about fifty acres in extent, rising to within five fathoms of the surface of the sea. This spot is the resort of incredible numbers of fish, both deep-sea haunting and surface swimming. Some of the latter, such as the *pala* (not the *palu*)--a long, scaleless, beautifully-formed fish, with a head of bony plates and teeth like a rip-saw--are of great size, and afford splendid sport, as they are game fighters and almost as powerful as a porpoise. They run to over 100 lbs., and yet are by no means a coarse fish. In the shallow water on the top of this mountain reef there are some eight or nine varieties of rock cod, none of which were of any great size; but far below, at a depth of from fifty to seventy fathoms, there were some truly monstrous fish of this species, and I and my missionary friend had the luck to catch the four largest ever taken--221 lbs., 208 lbs., 118 lbs., and 111 lbs. I had caught when fishing for schnapper, in thirty fathoms off Camden Haven, on the coast of New South Wales, a mottled black and grey rock cod, which weighed 83 lbs., and was assured by the Sydney Museum authorities that such a weight for a rock cod was rare in that part of the Pacific, but that *beche-de-mer* fishermen on the Great Barrier Reef had occasionally captured fish of the same variety of double that size and weight.

Not possessing a boat, we fished from a canoe--a light, but strong and beautifully constructed craft, with "whalebacks" fore and aft to keep it from being swamped by seas when facing or running from a surf. The outrigger was formed of a very light wood, called *pua*, about fourteen inches in circumference. With the teacher and myself there usually went with us a third man, whose duty it was to keep the canoe head to wind, for anchoring in deep water in such a tiny craft was out of the question, as well as dangerous, should a heavy fish or a shark get foul of the outrigger. Capsizes in the daytime we did not mind, but at night numbers of grey sharks were always cruising around, and they were then especially savage and daring.

Leaving the pretty little village, which was embowered in a palm grove on the lee side of the island, we would, if intending to fish on the Tia Kau, make a start before dawn, remain there till the canoe was loaded to her raised gunwale pieces with the weight of fish, and then return. Night fishing on the Tia Kau by a single canoe was forbidden by the *kaupule* (head men) as being too dangerous on account of the sharks, and so usually from ten to twenty canoes set out together. If one did come to grief through being swamped, or capsized by having the outrigger fouled by a shark, there was always assistance near at hand, and it rarely happened that any of the crew were bitten. In 1872, however, a fearful tragedy occurred on the Tia Kau, when a party of seventy natives--men, women, and children--who were crossing to the neighbouring Island of Nanomea, were attacked by sharks when overtaken on the reef by a squall at night. Only two escaped to tell the tale.[14]

If, however, we meant to try for *takuo*, a huge variety of the mackerel-tribe, or *lahe'u*, a magnificent bream-shaped fish, we had no need to go so far as the dangerous Tia Kau; three or four cable-lengths from the beach, and right in front of the village, we could lie in water as smooth as glass, and seventy fathoms in depth. Our bait was invariably flying-fish, freshly caught, or the tentacles of an octopus. My lines were of white American cotton, and I generally used two hooks, one below and one above the sinker, both baited with a whole flying-fish, while my companions preferred wooden or iron hooks, of their own manufacture, and lines made from hibiscus bark or coconut fibre.

I shall always remember with pleasure my first *lahe'u*. I was accompanied by the native teacher alone, and we paddled off from the village just after evening service, and brought to about a quarter of a mile outside the reef. The rest of the islanders had gone round in their canoes to the weather side of the little island to fish for *takuo*, for we were expecting a *malaga*, or party of visitors from the Island of Nukufetau in a day or two, and unusual supplies of fish had to be obtained, to sustain, not only the island's record as the fishing centre of the universe, but the people's reputation for hospitality. It had been my suggestion to the teacher that he and I, who were unable to accompany the others, should try what we could do nearer home. The night was brilliantly starlight, and the sea as smooth as glass--so smooth that there was not even the faintest swell upon the reef. The trade wind was at rest, and not the faintest breath of air moved the foliage of the coco palms lining the white strip of beach. Now and then a splash or a sudden commotion in the water around us would denote that some hapless flying-fish had taken an aerial flight from a pursuing *pala*, or that a shark had seized a turtle in his cruel jaws. Lighting our pipes, we lowered our lines together according to island etiquette, and touched bottom at thirty fathoms; then hauled in a fathom or two of line to avoid fouling the coral. In a few minutes my companion hooked an *utu*, a sluggish fish, somewhat like a salmon in appearance, with shining silvery scales and a broad flat head. As he was hauling in, and I was looking over the side of the canoe to watch it coming up, I felt a sharp, heavy tug at my own line, and, before I could check it, thirty or forty yards of line whizzed through my fingers with lightning speed.

"*Lahe'u!*" shouted the teacher, hurriedly making his own line fast, and whipping up his paddle. "Don't give out any more line or he will run under the reef, and we shall lose him."

I knew by the vibration and hum of the line as soon as I had it well in hand that there was a heavy and powerful fish at the end. Ioane, disregarding the *utu* as being of no importance in comparison to a *lahe'u*, was plunging his paddle rapidly into the water, and endeavouring to back the canoe seaward into deeper water, but, in spite of his efforts and my own, we were being taken quickly inshore. For some two or three minutes the canoe was dragged steadily landward, and I knew that once the *lahe'u* succeeded in getting underneath the overhanging ledge of reef, there would be but little chance of our taking him except by diving, and diving on a moonless night under a reef, and freeing a fish from jagged branches of coral, is not a pleasant task, although an Ellice Islander does not much mind it. Finding that I could not possibly turn the fish, I asked Ioane what I should do. He told me to let go a few fathoms of line, brace my knee against the thwart, and then trust to the sudden jerk to cant the fish's head one way or the other. I did as I was told. Out flew the line, and then came a shock that made the canoe fairly jump, lifted the outrigger clear out of the water, and all but capsized her. But the ruse was successful, for, with a furious shake, *lahe'u* changed his course, and started off at a tremendous rate, parallel with the reef, and then gradually headed seaward.

"Let him go," said Ioane, who was carefully watching the tautened-out line, and steering at the same time. "'Tis a strong fish, but he is ***man tonu*** (truly hooked), and will now tire. But give him no more line, and haul up to him."

For fully five minutes the canoe went flying over the water, and I continued to haul in line fathom by fathom, until I caught sight of, deep down in the water right ahead, a great phosphorescent boil and bubble. Then the pace began to slacken, as the gallant fighter began to turn from side to side, shaking his head and making futile breaks from port to starboard. Bidding me come amidships with the line, Ioane took in his paddle, and picked up the harpoon which we always carried on the outrigger platform in case of meeting a turtle. Nearer and nearer came the great fish, till, with a splash of phosphorescent light and spray, he came to the surface, beating the water with his forked and bony tail, and still trying to get a chance for another downward run. Then Ioane, waiting his opportunity, sent the iron clean through him from side to side, and I sat down and watched, with a thrill of satisfaction and a sigh of relief, his final flurry. In a few minutes we hauled him alongside, drew the harpoon, and with some difficulty managed to get him over the side and lower him into the bottom of the canoe amidships, where he lay fore and aft, his curved back standing up nearly a foot and a half above the raised gunwale. Although not above four feet in length, he was nearly three in depth, and about sixteen inches thick at the shoulder--a truly noble fish.

"We have done well," said the teacher, with a pleased laugh, as he hauled in his own line and dropped a 6-lb. *utu* into the canoe. "There will be much talk over this to-morrow, for these people here are very conceited, and think that no one but themselves can catch *lahe'u* and *pala*. They will know better now, when they see this one."

We returned to the shore within two hours from the time we left, with my *lahe'u*, an *utu*, and five or six salmon-like fish called *tau-tau*, all nocturnal feeders, and all highly thought of by the natives, especially the latter. The *lahe'u* we hung up under the missionary's verandah, and at daylight I had the intense satisfaction of seeing a crowd of natives surrounding it, and of hearing their flattering allusions to myself as a *papalagi masani tonu futi ika*--a white man who really could fish like a native.

On a Tidal River

The English visitor to the Eastern Colonies of Australia who is in search of sport with either rod or hand line can always obtain excellent fishing in the summer months even in such traffic-disturbed harbours as Sydney, Newcastle, and other ports; but on the tidal rivers of the eastern and southern seaboard he can, every day, catch more fish than he can carry during seven months of the year. In the true winter months deep sea fishing is not much favoured, except during the prevalence of westerly winds, when, for days at a time, the Pacific is as smooth as a lake; but in the rivers, from Mallacoota Inlet, which is a few miles over the Victorian boundary, to the Tweed River on the north of New South Wales, the stranger may fairly revel not only in the delights of splendid fishing but in the charms of beautiful scenery. He needs no guide, will be put to but little expense, for the country hotel accommodation is good and cheap; and, should he visit some of the northern rivers where the towns, or rather small settlements, are few and far between, he will find the settlers the embodiment of British hospitality.

Some three years ago the writer formed one of the crew of a little steamer of fifty tons named the *Jenny Lind*, which was sent out along the coast in the endeavour to revive the coast whaling industry. Through stress of weather we had frequently to make a dash for shelter, towing our sole whaleboat, to one of the many tidal rivers on the coast between Sydney and Gabo Island. Here we would remain until the weather broke, and our crew would literally cover the deck with an extraordinary variety of fish in the course of a few hours. Then, at low tide, we could always fill a couple of cornsacks with excellent oysters, and get bucketfuls of large prawns by means of a scoop net improvised from a piece of mosquito netting; game, too, was very plentiful on the lagoons. The settlers were generally glad to see us, and gave us so freely of milk, butter, pumpkins, &c., that, despite the rough handling we always got at sea from the weather, we grew quite fat. But as the greater part of my fishing experience was gained on the northern rivers of the colony of N.S. Wales it is of them I shall write.

Eighteen hours' run by steamer from Sydney is the Hastings River, on the southern bank of which, a mile from the bar, is the old-time town of Port Macquarie, a quaint, sleepy little place of six hundred inhabitants, who spend their days in fishing and sleeping and waiting for better times. There are two or three fairly good hotels, very pretty scenery along the coast and up the river, and a stranger can pass a month without suffering from ennui--that is, of course, if he be fond of fishing and shooting; if he is not he should avoid going there, for it is the dullest coast town in New South Wales. The southern shore, from the steamer wharf to opposite the bar, is lined with a hard beach, on which at high tide, or slack water at low tide, one may sit down in comfort and have great sport with bream, whiting, and flathead. As soon as the tide turns, however, and is well on the ebb or flow, further fishing is impossible, for the river rushes out to sea with great velocity, and the incoming tide is almost as swift. On the other side of the harbour is a long, sandy point, called the North Shore, about a mile in length. This, at the north end, is met by a somewhat dense scrub, which lines the right bank of the river for a couple of miles, and affords a splendid shade to any one fishing on the river bank. The outer or ocean beach is but a few minutes' walk from the river, and a magnificent beach it is, trending in one great unbroken curve to Point Plomer, seven miles from the township.

Before ascending the river on a fishing trip one has to provide one's self with a plentiful supply of cockles, or "pippies," as they are called locally. These can only be obtained on the northern ocean beach, and not the least enjoyable part of a day's sport consists in getting them. They are triangular in shape, with smooth shells of every imaginable colour, though a rich purple is commonest. As the back wash leaves the sands bare these bivalves may be seen in thick but irregular patches protruding from the sand. Sometimes, if the tide is not low enough, one may get rolled over by the surf if he happen to have his back turned seaward. Generally I was accompanied by two boys, known as "Condon's Twins." They were my landlord's sons, and certainly two of the smartest young sportsmen--although only twelve years old--ever met with. Both were very small for their age, and I was always in doubt as to which was which. They were always delighted to come with me, and did not mind being soused by a roller now and then when filling my "pippy" bag. Pippies are the best bait one can have for whiting (except prawns) in Australia, for, unlike the English whiting, it will not touch fish bait of any sort, although, when very hungry, it will sometimes take to octopus flesh. Bream (whether black or silvery), flathead, trevally, jew-fish, and, indeed, all other fish obtained in Australia, are not so dainty, for, although they like "pippies" and prawns best, they will take raw meat, fish, or octopus bait with readiness. Certain species of sea and river mullet are like them in this respect, and good sport may be had from them with a rod in the hot months, as Dick and Fred, the twins aforesaid, well knew, for often would their irate father wrathfully ask them why they wasted their time catching "them worthless mullet."

But let me give an idea of one of many days' fishing on the Hastings, spent with the "Twins." Having filled a sugar bag with "pippies" on the ocean beach, we put on our boots and make our way through the belt of scrub to where our boat is lying, tied to the protruding roots of a tree. Each of us is armed with a green stick, and we pick our way pretty carefully, for black snakes are plentiful, and to tread on one may mean death. The density of the foliage overhead is such that but little sunlight can pierce through it, and the ground is soft to our feet with the thick carpet of fallen leaves beneath. No sound but the murmuring of the sea and the hoarse notes of countless gulls breaks the silence, for this side of the river is uninhabited, and its solitude disturbed only by some settler who has ridden down the coast to look for straying cattle, or by a fishing party from the town. Our boat, which we had hauled up and then tied to the tree, is now afloat, for the tide has risen, and the long stretches of yellow sandbanks which line the channel on the farther side are covered now with a foot of water. As we drift up the river, eating our lunch, and letting the boat take care of herself, a huge, misshapen thing comes round a low point, emitting horrid groanings and wheezings. It is a steam stern-wheel punt, loaded with mighty logs of black-butt and tallow wood, from fifty feet to seventy feet in length, cut far up the Hastings and the Maria and Wilson Rivers, and destined for the sawmill at Port Macquarie.

In another hour we are at our landing-place, a selector's abandoned homestead, built of rough slabs, and standing about fifty yards back from the river and the narrow line of brown, winding beach. The roof had long since fallen in, and the fences and outbuildings lay low, covered with vines and creepers. The intense solitude of the place, the motionless forest of lofty grey-boled swamp gums that encompassed it on all sides but one, and the wide stretch of river before it were calculated to inspire melancholy in any one but an ardent fisherman. Scarcely have we hauled our boat up on the sand, and deposited our provisions and water in the roofless house, when we hear a commotion in the river--a swarm of fish called "tailer" are making havoc among a "school" of small mullet, many of which fling themselves out upon the sand. Presently all is quiet again, and we get our lines ready.

For whiting and silvery bream rather fine lines are used, but we each have a heavy line for flathead, for these fish are caught in the tidal rivers on a sandy bottom up to three feet and four feet in length. They are in colour, both on back and belly, much like a sole, of great width across the shoulders, and then taper away to a very fine tail. The head is perfectly flat, very thin, and armed on each side with very sharp bones pointing tailward; a wound from one of these causes intense inflammation. The fins are small--so small as to appear almost rudimentary--yet the fish swims, or rather darts, along the bottom with amazing rapidity. They love to lie along the banks a few feet from the shore, where, concealed in the sand, they can dart out upon and seize their prey in their enormous "gripsack" mouths. The approach of a boat or a person walking along the sand will cause them to at once speed like lightning into deep water, leaving behind them a wake of sand and mud which is washed off their backs in their flight. Still, although not a pleasing fish to look at, the flathead is of a delicious and delicate flavour. There are some variations in their shades of colour, from a pale, delicate grey to a very dark brown, according to their habitat, and, although most frequent in very shallow water, they are often caught in great quantities off the coast in from ten to fifteen fathoms of water. Gut or wire snoodings are indispensable when fishing for flathead, else the fish invariably severs the line with his fine needle-pointed teeth, which are set very closely together. Nothing comes amiss to them as food, but they have a great love for small mullet or whiting, or a piece of octopus tentacle.

Baiting our heavy lines with mullet--two hooks with brass-wire snoods to each line--we throw out about thirty yards, then, leaving two or three fathoms loose upon the shore, we each thrust a stick firmly into the sand, and take a turn of the line round it. As the largest flathead invariably dart upon the bait, and then make a bolt with it, this plan is a good one to follow, unless, of course, they are biting freely; in that case the smaller lines for bream and whiting, &c., are hauled in, for there is more real sport in landing an 8-lb. flathead than there is in catching smaller fish, for he is very game, and fights fiercely for his life.

Having disposed our big lines, we bait the smaller ones with "pippies," and not two minutes at the outside elapse after the sinkers have touched bottom when we know we are to have a good time, for each of us has hooked a fish, and three whiting are kicking on the sand before five minutes have expired. Then for another hour we throw out and haul in again as quickly as possible, landing whiting from 6 oz. to nearly 2 lbs. in weight. One of the "Twins" has three hooks on his line, and occasionally lands three fish together, and now and again we get small bream and an occasional "tailer" of 2 lbs. or 3 lbs. As the sun mounts higher the breeze dies away, the heat becomes very great, and we have frequent recourse to our water jar--in one case mixing it with whisky. Then the whiting cease to bite as suddenly as they have begun, and move off into deeper water. Just as we are debating as to whether we shall take the boat out into mid-stream, Twin Dick gives a yell as his stick is suddenly whipped out of the sand, and the loose line lying beside it rushes away into the water. But Dick is an old hand, and lets his fish have his first bolt, and then turns him. "By Jingo! sir, he's a big fellow," he cries, as he hauls in, the line now as taut as a telegraph wire, and then the other twin comes to his aid, and in a few minutes the outline of the fish is seen, coming in straight ahead as quick as they can pull him. When he is within ten feet of the beach the boys run up the bank and land him safely, as he turns his body into a circle in his attempts to shake out the hook. Being called upon to estimate his weight, I give it as 11 lbs., much to the twins' sorrow--they think it 15 lbs.

Half an hour passes, and we catch but half a dozen silvery bream and some small baby whiting, for now the sun is beating down upon our heads, and our naked feet begin to burn and sting, so we adjourn to the old house and rest awhile, leaving our big lines securely tied. But, though the breeze for which we wait comes along by two o'clock, the fish do not, and so, after disinterring our takes from the wet sand wherein we had buried them as caught to prevent them being spoilt by the sun, we get aboard again and pull across to the opposite bank of the river. Here, in much deeper water, about fifteen feet right under the clayey bank, we can see hundreds of fine bream, and now and then some small jew-fish. Taking off our sinkers, we have as good and more exciting sport among the bream than we had with the whiting, catching between four and five dozen by six o'clock. Then, after boiling the billy and eating some fearfully tough corned meat, we get into the boat again, hoist our sail, and land at the little township just after dark.

Such was one of many similar day's sport on the Hastings, which, with the Bellinger, the Nambucca, the Macleay, and the Clarence, affords good fishing practically all the year round. Then, besides these tidal rivers, there are at frequent intervals along the coast tidal lagoons and "blind" creeks where fish congregate in really incredible quantities. Such places as Lake Illawarra and Lake Macquarie are fishing resorts well known to the tourist; but along the northern coast, where the population is scantier, and access by rail or steamer more difficult, there is an absolutely new field open to the sportsman--in fact, these places are seldom visited for either fishing or shooting by people from Sydney. During November and December the bars of these rivers are literally black with incredible numbers of coarse sea-salmon--a fish much like the English sea-bass--which, making their way over the bars, swim up the rivers and remain there for about a week. Although these fish, which weigh from 6 lbs. to 10 lbs., do not take a bait and are rather too coarse to eat, their roes are very good, especially when smoked. They are captured with the greatest of ease, either by spearing or by the hand; for sometimes they are in such dense masses that they are unable to manoeuvre in small bays; and the urchins of coastal towns hail their yearly advent with delight. They usually make their first appearance about the second week in November, and are always followed by a great number of very large sharks and saw-fish, which commit dreadful havoc in their serried and helpless ranks. Following the sea-salmon, the rivers are next visited in January by shoals of very large sea-mullet--blue-black backs, silvery bellies and sides, and yellow fins and tails. These, too, will not take a bait, but are caught in nets, and, if a steamer happens to be on the eve of leaving for Sydney, many hundreds of baskets are sent away; but they barely pay the cost of freight and commission, I believe. There are several varieties of sea-mullet, one or two of which will take the hook freely, and I have often caught them off the rocky coast of New South Wales with a rod when the sea has been smooth. The arrival of the big sea-mullet denotes that the season for jew-fish is at its height; and if the stranger to Australian waters wants exciting sport let him try jew-fishing at night. In deep water off the coast these great fish are occasionally caught during daylight, but a dull, cloudy night is best, when they may be caught from the beach or river bank in shallow water. Very stout lines and heavy hooks are used, for a 90-lb. or l00-lb. jew-fish is very common. Baiting with a whole mullet or whiting, or one of the tentacles of an octopus, the most amateurish fisherman cannot fail to hook two or three jew-fish in a night. (Even in Sydney harbour I have seen some very large ones caught by people fishing from ferry wharves.) They are very powerful, and also very game, and when they rise to the surface make a terrific splashing. At one place on the Hastings River, called Blackman's Point, a party of four of us took thirteen fish, the heaviest of which was 42 lbs. and the lightest 9 lbs. Next morning, however, the Blackman's Point ferryman, who always set a line from his punt when he turned in, showed us one of over 70 lbs. When they grow to such a size as this they are not eaten locally, as the flesh is very often full of thin, thread-like worms. The young fish, however, are very palatable.

The saw-fish, to which I have before alluded as harrying the swarms of sea-salmon, also make havoc with the jew-fish, and very often are caught on jew-fish lines. They are terrible customers to get foul of (I do not confound them with the sword-fish) when fishing from a small boat. Their huge bone bill, set on both sides with its terrible sharp spikes, their great length, and enormous strength, render it impossible to even get them alongside, and there is no help for it but either to cut the line or pull up anchor and land the creature on the shore. Even then the task of despatching one of these fish is no child's play on a dark night, for they lash their long tails about with such fury that a broken leg might be the result of coming too close. In the rivers of Northern Queensland the saw-fish attain an enormous size, and the Chinese fishermen about Cooktown and Townsville often have their nets destroyed by a saw-fish enfolding himself in them. Alligators, by the way, do the same thing there, and are sometimes captured, perfectly helpless, in the folds of the nets, in which they have rolled themselves over and over again, tearing it beyond repair with their feet, but eventually yielding to their fate.

The schnapper, the best of all Australian fish, is too well known to English visitors to describe in detail. Most town-bred Australians generally regard it as a purely ocean-loving fish, or at least only frequenting very deep waters in deep harbours, such as Sydney, Jervis Bay, and Twofold Bay. This is quite a mistake, for in many of the rivers, twenty or more miles up from the sea, the writer and many other people have not only caught these beautiful fish, but seen fishermen haul in their nets filled with them. But they seldom remain long, preferring the blue depths of ocean to the muddy bottoms of tidal rivers, for they are rock-haunting and surf-loving.

Of late years the northern bar harbours and rivers of New South Wales have been visited by a fish that in my boyhood's days was unknown even to the oldest fisherman--the bonito. Although in shape and size they exactly resemble the ocean bonito of tropic seas, these new arrivals are lighter in colour, with bands of marbled grey along the sides and belly. They bite freely at a running bait--*i.e.,* when a line is towed astern, and are very good when eaten quite fresh, but, like all of the mackerel tribe, rapidly deteriorate in a few hours after being caught. The majority of the coast settlers will not eat them, being under the idea that, as they are all but scaleless, they are "poisonous." This silly impression also prevails with regard to many other scaleless fish on the Australian coast, some of which, such as the trevally, are among the best and most delicate in flavour. The black and white rock cod is also regarded with aversion by the untutored settlers of the small coast settlements, yet these fish are sold in Sydney, like the schnapper, at prohibitive prices.

In conclusion, let me advise any one who is contemplating a visit to Australia, and means to devote any of his time to either river or sea fishing, to take his rods with him; all the rest of his tackle he can buy as cheap in the colonies as he can in England. Rods are but little used in salt-water fishing in Australia, and are rather expensive. Those who do use a rod are usually satisfied with a bamboo--a very good rod it makes, too, although inconvenient to carry when travelling--but the generality of people use hand lines. And the visitor must not be persuaded that he can always get good fishing without going some distance from Sydney or Melbourne. That there is some excellent sport to be obtained in Port Jackson in summer is true, but it is lacking in a very essential thing--the quietude that is dear to the heart of every true fisherman.

Denison Gets Another Ship

Owing to reduced circumstances, and a growing hatred of the hardships of the sea, young Tom Denison (ex-supercargo of the South Sea Island trading schooner *Palestine*) had sailed from Sydney to undertake the management of an alleged duck-farm in North Queensland. The ducks, and the vast area of desolation in which they suffered a brief existence, were the property of a Cooktown bank, the manager of which was Denison's brother. He was a kind-hearted man, who wanted to help Tom along in the world, and, therefore, was grieved when at the end of three weeks the latter came into Cooktown humping his swag, smoking a clay pipe, and looking exceedingly tired, dirty, and disreputable generally. However, all might have gone well even then had not Mrs. Aubrey Denison, the brother's wife, unduly interfered and lectured Tom on his "idle and dissolute life," as she called it, and made withering remarks about the low tastes of sailors other than captains of mail steamers or officers in the Navy. Tom, who intended to borrow L10 from his brother to pay his passage back to Sydney to look for a ship, bore it all in silence, and then said that he should like to give up the sea and become a missionary in the South Seas, where he was "well acquainted with the natives."

Mrs. Aubrey (who was a very refined young lady) smiled contemptuously, and turned down the corners of her pretty little mouth in a manner that made the unsuccessful duck-farmer boil with suppressed fury, as she remarked that *she* had heard of some of the shocking stories he had been telling the accountant and cashier of the *characters* of the people in the South Seas, and *she* quite understood *why* he wished to return there and re-associate with his vulgar and wicked companions. Now, she added, had he stuck bravely to work with the ducks, the Bank (she uttered the word "Bank" in the tone of reverence as one would say "The Almighty") would have watched his career with interest, and in time his brother would have used his influence with the General Manager to obtain a position for him, Tom Denison, in the Bank itself! But, judging from *her* knowledge of his (Tom's) habits and disposition, she would be doing wrong to hold out the slightest hope for him now, and------

"Look here, Maud, you're only twenty-two--two years older than me, and you talk like an old grandmother;" and then his wrath overpowered his judgment--"and you'll look like one before you're twenty-five. Don't you lecture *me*. I'm not your husband, *thank Heaven above*! And damn the bank and its carmine ducks." (He did not say "carmine," but I study the proprieties, and this is not a sanguinary story.)

From the weatherboard portals of the bank Tom strode out in undisguised anger, and obtained employment on a collier, discharging coals. Then, by an extraordinary piece of good luck, he got a billet as proof-reader on the North Queensland *Trumpet Call*, from which, after an exciting three weeks, he was dismissed for "general incompetency and wilful neglect of his duties." So with sorrow in his heart he had turned to the ever-resourceful sea again for a living. He worked his passage down to Sydney in an old, heart-broken, wheezing steamer named the *You Yangs*, and stepped jauntily ashore with sixteen shillings in his pocket, some little personal luggage rolled up in his blanket, and an unlimited confidence in his own luck.

Two vessels were due from the South Sea Islands in about a month, and as the skippers were both well known to and were on friendly terms with him, he felt pretty certain of getting a berth as second mate or supercargo on one of them. Then he went to look for a quiet lodging.

This was soon found, and then realising the fact that sixteen shillings would not permit him viewing the sights of Sydney and calling upon the Governor, as is the usual procedure with intellectual and dead-broke Englishmen who come to Australia with letters of introduction from people who are anxious to get rid of them, he tried to get temporary employment by applying personally at the leading warehouses and merchants' offices. The first day he failed; also the second. On the third day the secretary of a milk company desired him to call again in three days. He did, and was then told by the manager that he "might have something" for him in a month or two. This annoyed Tom, as he had put on his sole clean collar that morning to produce a good impression. He asked the official if six months would not suit him better, as he wanted to go away on a lengthy fishing trip with the Attorney-General. The manager looked at him in a dignified manner, and then bade him an abrupt good-day.

A week passed. Funds were getting low. Eight shillings had been paid in advance for his room, and he had spent five in meals. But he was not despondent; the ***Susannah Booth***, dear, comfortable old wave-puncher, beloved of hard-up supercargoes, was due in a week, and, provided he could inspire his landlady with confidence until then, all would be well.

But the day came when he had to spend his last shilling, and after a fruitless endeavour to get a job on the wharves to drive one of the many steam winches at work discharging cargo from the various ships, he returned home in disgust.

That night, as he sat cogitating in his bedroom over his lucklessness, his eye fell on a vegetable monstrosity from Queensland, presented to him by one of the hands on board the ***You Yangs***. It was a huge, dried bean-pod, about four feet long, and contained about a dozen large black beans, each about the size of a watch. He had seen these beans, after the kernels were scooped out, mounted with silver, and used as match-boxes by bushmen and other Australian gentry. It at once occurred to him that he might sell it. Surely the thing ought to be worth at least five shillings.

In two minutes he was out in the street, but to his disgust found most of the shops closed, except the very small retail establishments.

Entering a little grocery store, he approached the proprietor, a man with a pale, gargoyle-like face, and unpleasant-looking, raggedy teeth, and showing him the bean, asked him to buy it.

The merchant looked at it with some interest and asked Tom what it was called.

Tom said it was a ***Locomotor Ataxy***. (He didn't know what a ***locomotor ataxy*** was; but it sounded well, and was all the Latin he knew, having heard from his mother that a dissolute brother of hers had been afflicted with that complaint, superinduced by spirituous liquors.)

The grocer-man turned the vegetable over and over again in his hand, and then asked the would-be vendor if he had any more. Tom said he hadn't. The ***locomotor ataxy***, he remarked, was a very rare bean, and very valuable. But he would sell it cheap--for five shillings.

"Don't want it," said the man rudely, pushing it away contemptuously. "It's only a faked-up thing anyway, made of paper-mashy."

Tom tried to convince him that the thing was perfectly genuine, and actually grew on a vine in North Queensland; but the Notre Dame gargoyle-featured person only heard him with a snort of contempt. It was obvious he wouldn't buy it. So, sneeringly observing to the grocer that no doubt five shillings was a large sum for a man in such a small way of business as he was, Tom went out again into the cold world.

He tried several other places, but no one would even look at the thing. After vainly tramping about for over two hours, he turned away towards his lodging, feeling very dispirited, and thinking about breakfast.

Turning up a side street called Queen's Place, so as to make a short cut home, he espied in a dimly-lighted little shop an old man and a boy working at the cobbler trade. They had honest, intelligent faces, and looked as if they wanted to buy a *locomotor ataxy* very badly. He tapped at the door and then entered.

"Would you like to buy this?" he said to the old man. He did not like to repeat his foolish Latin nonsense, for the old fellow had such a worn, kindly face, and his honest, searching eyes met his in such a way that he felt ashamed to ask him to buy what could only be worthless rubbish to him.

The cobbler looked at the monstrosity wonderingly. "'Tis a rare big bean," he said, in the trembling quaver of old age, and with a mumbling laugh like that of a pleased child. "I'll give you two shillin's for it. I suppose you want money badly, or else you wouldn't be wanderin' about at ten o'clock at night tryin' to sell it. I hope you come by it honest, young man?"

Tom satisfied him on this score, and then the ancient gave him the two shillings. Bidding him good-night, Tom returned home and went to bed.

(Quite two years after, when Denison returned to Sydney from the South Seas with more money "than was good for his moral welfare," as his sister-in-law remarked, he sought out the old cobbler gentleman and bought back his *locomotor ataxy* bean for as many sovereigns as he had been given shillings for it.)

Next morning he was down at the wharves before six o'clock, smoking his pipe contentedly, after breakfasting sumptuously at a coffee-stall for sixpence. There was a little American barque lying alongside the Circular Quay, and some of the hands were bending on her head-sails. Tom sat down on the wharf stringer dangling his feet and watching them intently. Presently the mate appeared on the poop, smoking a cigar. He looked at Tom critically for a moment or so, and then said--

"Looking for a ship, young feller?"

The moment Tom heard him speak, he jumped to his feet, for he knew the voice, last heard when the possessor of it was mate of the island trading schooner *Sadie Caller*, a year before in Samoa.

"Is that you, Bannister?" he cried.

"Reckon 'taint no one else, young feller. Why, Tom Denison, is it you? Step right aboard."

Tom was on the poop in an instant, the mate coming to him with outstretched hand.

"What's the matter, Tom? Broke?"

"Stony!"

"Sit down here and tell me all about it. I heard you had left the *Palestine*. Say, sling that dirty old pipe overboard, and take one of these cigars. The skipper will be on deck presently, and the sight of it would rile him terrible. He hez his new wife aboard, and she considers pipes ez low-down."

Tom laughed as he thought of Mrs. Aubrey, and flung his clay over the side. "What ship is this, Bannister?"

"The *J. W. Seaver*, of 'Frisco. We're from the Gilbert Islands with a cargo of copra."

"Who is your supercargo?"

"Haven't got one. Can't get one here, either. Say, Tom, you're the man. The captain will jump at getting you! Since he married he considers his life too valuable to be trusted among natives, and funks at going ashore and doing supercargo's work. Now you come below, and I'll rake out enough money to get you a high-class suit of store clothes and shiny boots. Then you come back to dinner. I'll talk to him between then and now. He knows a lot about you. I'll tell him that since you left the *Palestine* you've been touring your native country to 'expand your mind.' *She's* Boston, as ugly as a brown stone jug, and highly intellectual. *He's* all right, and as good a sailor-man as ever trod a deck, but *she's* boss, runs the ship, and looks after the crew's morals. Thet's why we're short-handed. But she'll take to you like lightning--when she hears that you've been 'expanding your mind.' Buy a second-hand copy of Longfellow's, poems, and tell her that it has been your constant companion in all your wanderings among vicious cannibals, and she'll just decorate your cabin like a prima-donna's boudoir, darn your socks, and make you read some of her own poetry."

That afternoon, Mr. Thomas Denison, clean-shirted and looking eminently respectable and prosperous, and feeling once more a man after the degrading duck episode in North Queensland, was strolling about George Street with Bannister, and at peace with the world and himself. For the skipper's wife had been impressed with his intellectuality and modest demeanour, and was already at work decorating his cabin--as Bannister had prophesied.

Jack Shark's Pilot

Early one morning as we in the ***Palestine***, South Sea trading schooner, were sailing slowly between Fotuna and Alofa--two islands lying to the northward of Fiji--one of the native hands came aft and reported two large sharks alongside. The mate at once dived below for his shark hook, while I tried to find a suitable bit of beef in the harness cask. Just as the mate appeared carrying the heavy hook and chain, our skipper, who was lying on the skylight smoking his pipe, although half asleep, inquired if there were "any pilot fish with the brutes."

"Yes, sir," said a sailor who was standing in the waist, looking over the side, "there's quite a lot of 'em. I've never seen so many at one time before. There's nigh on a dozen."

The captain was on his feet in an instant. "Don't lower that hook of yours just yet, Porter," he said to the mate. "I'm going to get those pilot fish first. Tom, bring me up my small fishing line."

"They won't take a hook, will they?" I inquired.

"Just you wait and see, sonny. Ever taste pilot fish?"

"No. Are they good to eat?"

"Best fish in the ocean, barring flying-fish," replied the skipper, as, after examining his line, he cut off both hook and leaden sinker and bent on a small-sized ***pa***--a native-made bonito hook cut out from a solid piece of pearl-shell.

Then jumping up into the whaleboat which hung in davits on the starboard quarter he waited for the sharks to appear, and the mate and I leant over the side and watched. We had not long to wait, for in a few minutes one came swimming quickly up from astern, and was almost immediately joined by the other, which had been hanging about amidships. They were both, however, pretty deep down, and at first I could not discern any pilot fish. The captain, however, made a cast and the hook dropped in the water, about fifty feet in the rear of the sharks; he let it sink for less than half a minute, and then began hauling in the line as quickly as possible, and at the same moment I saw some of the pilot fish quite distinctly--some swimming alongside and some just ahead of their detestable companions, which were now right under the counter. Then something gleamed brightly, and the shining hook appeared, for a second or two only, for two of the "pilots" darted after it with lightning-like rapidity, and presently one came to the surface with a splash, beautifully hooked, and was swung up into the boat.

"Now for some fun," cried the captain, as tossing the fish to us on deck he again lowered the hook. This time it had barely touched the surface of the water when away went the line with a rush right under our keel.

"This is a big fellow," said the skipper, and up came another dark blue and silver beauty about a foot in length, dropping off the hook just in time as he was hoisted clear of the gunwale. Then, in less than ten minutes--so eager were they to rush the hook the moment it struck the water--five more were jumping about upon the deck or in the boat. Then came a calamity, the eighth fish dropped off when half way up and took the hook with him, having swallowed it and bitten through the line.

The captain jumped on deck again and began rooting out his bag for another small-sized *pa*, but to his disgust could not find one ready for use--none of them having the actual "hook" portion lashed to the shank, and the operation of lashing one of these cleverly-made native hooks takes some little time and patience, for the holes which are bored through the base of the "hook" part in order to lash it to the shank are very small, and only very fine and strong cord, such as banana-fibre, can be used. However, while the irate captain was fussing over his task, the mate and I were watching the movements of the sharks and their little friends with the greatest interest, having promised the captain not to lower the shark hook till he had caught the rest of the pilot fish, for he assured us that they would most likely disappear after the sharks were captured. (I learned from my own experience afterward that he was mistaken, for when a shark is caught at sea his attendants will frequently remain with the ship for weeks, or until another shark appears, in which case they at once attach themselves to him.)

Both sharks were now swimming almost on the surface, so close to the ship that they could have been caught in a running bowline or harpooned with the greatest ease; and in fact our native crew, who were very partial to shark's flesh, had both harpoon and bowline in readiness in case the cunning brutes would not take a bait. They were both of great size--the largest being over twelve or thirteen feet in length. With the smaller one were three pilot fish, one swimming directly under the end of its nose, the others just over its eyes; the larger had but one attendant, which kept continually changing its position, sometimes being on one side, then on another, then disappearing for a few moments underneath the monster's belly, or pressing itself so closely against the creature's side that it appeared as if it was adhering to it. I had never before seen these fish at such close quarters, and their extraordinary activity and seeming attachment to their savage companions was most astonishing to witness; occasionally when either of the sharks would cease moving, they would take up a position within a few inches of its jaws, remain there a few seconds, and then swim under its belly and reappear at the tail, then slowly make their way along its back or sides to the hideous head again. Sometimes, either singly or all together, they would dart away on either side, but quickly returned, never being absent more than a minute. These brief excursions showed them to be extremely swift, yet when they returned to their huge companions they instantly became--at least to all appearance--intensely sluggish and languid in their movements, and swam in an undecided, indefinite sort of manner as if thoroughly exhausted. But this was but in appearance, for suddenly they would again shoot away along the surface of the water with lightning-like rapidity, disappear from view of the keenest eye, and, ere you could count five, again be beside the vessel swimming as leisurely, if not as lazily, as if they were incapable of quickening their speed.

Having his line ready again, the captain now began fishing from the stern, and succeeded in catching three of the remaining four, the last one (which our natives said was the fish which had swallowed the first hook) refusing even to look at the tempting bit of iridescent pearl-shell. Then the impatient mate lowered his bait over the stern, having first passed the line outboard and given the end to three or four of the crew, who stood in the waist ready to haul in. The smaller of the two sharks was at once hooked, and when dragged up alongside amidships struggled and lashed about so furiously that the big fellow came lumbering up to see what was the matter, and Billy Rotumah, our native boatswain, who was watching for him, promptly drove a harpoon socket deeply into him between the shoulders; then, after some difficulty, a couple of running bowlines settled them both in a comfortable position to be stunned with an axe.

The schooner was at this time within a few miles of a small village on Alofa, named Mua, and presently a boat manned by natives boarded us to sell yams, taro, pineapples, and bananas, all of which we bought from them in exchange for the sharks' livers and some huge pieces of flesh weighing two or three hundred pounds. These people (who resemble the Samoans in appearance and language) were much impressed and terrified when they saw the pilot fish which had been caught, and told our crew that ours would be an unlucky ship--that we had done a dangerous and foolish thing. Their feeling on the subject was strong; for when I asked them if they would take two or three of the fish on shore to Father Herve, one of the French priests living on Fotuna, who was an old friend, they started back in mingled terror and indignation, and absolutely declined to even touch them. Taking one of the pilot fish up I held it by the head between my forefinger and thumb and asked the natives if they did not consider it good to look at.

"True," replied a fine, stalwart young fellow, speaking in Samoan, "it is good to look at," and then he added gravely, "Talofa lava ia te outou i le vaa nei, ua lata mai ne aso malaia ma le tiga|" ("Alas for all you people on this ship, there is a day of disaster and sorrow near you").

I tried to ascertain the cause of their terror, but could only elicit the statement that to kill a pilot fish meant direful misfortune. No sensible man, they asserted, would do such a senseless and *saua* (cruel) thing, and to eat one was an abomination unutterable.

As soon as our visitors had left I hurried to make a closer examination of our prizes before the cook took possession of them. Of the eleven, only one was over a foot in length, the rest ranged from five to ten inches. The beautiful dark blue of the head and along the back, so noticeable when first caught, had now lost its brilliancy, and the four wide vertical black stripes on the sides had also become dulled, although the silvery belly was still as bright as a new dollar. The eyes were rather large for such a small fish, and all the fins were blue-black, with a narrow white line running along the edges. Their appearance even an hour after death was very handsome, and in shape they were much like a very plump trout. In the stomachs of some we found small flying squid, little shrimps, and other Crustacea.

Our Manila-man cook, although not a genius, certainly knew how to fry fish, and that morning we had for breakfast some of Jack Shark's pilots--the most delicately-flavoured deep-sea fish I have ever tasted--except, perhaps, that wonderful and beautiful creature, the flying-fish.

The "Palu" of the Equatorial Pacific

During a residence of half a lifetime among the various island-groups of the North-western and South Pacific, I devoted much of my spare time--and I had plenty of it occasionally--to deep-sea fishing, my tutors being the natives of the Caroline, Marshall, Gilbert, and Ellice Groups.

The inhabitants of the last-named cluster of islands are, as I have said, the most skilled fishermen of all the Malayo-Polynesian peoples with whom it has been my fortune to have come in contact. The very poverty of their island homes--mere sandbanks covered with coconut and pandanus palms only--drives them to the sea for their food; for the Ellice Islanders, unlike their more fortunate prototypes who dwell in the forest-clad, mountainous, and fertile islands of Samoa, Tahiti, Raratonga, &c., live almost exclusively upon coconuts, the drupes of the pandanus palm, and fish. From their very infancy they look to the sea as the main source of their food-supply, either in the clear waters of the lagoon, among the breaking surf on the reef, or out in the blue depths of the ocean beyond. From morn till night the frail canoes of these semi-nude, brown-skinned, and fearless toilers of the sea may be seen by the voyager paddling swiftly over the rolling swell of the wide Pacific in chase of the **bonito**, or lying motionless upon the water, miles and miles away from the land, ground-fishing with lines a hundred fathoms long. Then, as the sun dips, the flare of torches will be seen along the sandy beaches as the night-seekers of flying-fish launch their canoes and urge them through the rolling surf beyond the reef, where, for perhaps three or four hours, they will paddle slowly to and fro, just outside the white line of roaring breakers, and return to the shore with their tiny craft half-filled with the most beautiful and wonderful fish in the world. The Ellice Island method of catching flying-fish would take too long to explain here, much as I should like to do so; my purpose is to describe a very remarkable fish called the ***palu***, in the capture of which these people are the most skilful. The catching of flying-fish, however, bears somewhat on the subject of this article, as the ***palu*** will not take any other bait but a flying-fish, and therefore a supply of the former is a necessary preliminary to ***palu*** fishing.

Let us imagine, then, that the bait has been secured, and that a party of ***palu***-fishers are ready to set out from the little island of Nanomaga, the smallest but most thickly populated of the Ellice Group. The night must be windless and moonless, the latter condition being absolutely indispensable, although, curiously enough, the fish will take the hook on an ordinary starlight night. Time after time have I tried my luck with either a growing or a waning moon, much to the amusement of the natives, and never once did I get a ***palu***, although other nocturnal-feeding fish bit freely enough.

The tackle used by the natives is made of coconut cinnet, four or eight-stranded, of great strength, and capable of holding a fifteen-foot shark should one of these prowlers seize the bait. The hook is made of wood--in fact, the same as is used for shark-fishing--about one inch and a half in diameter, fourteen inches in the shank, with a natural curve; the barb, or rather that which answers the purpose of a barb, being supplied by a small piece lashed horizontally across the top of the end of the curve. These peculiar wooden hooks are ***grown***; the roots of a tree called ***ngiia***, whose wood is of great toughness, are watched when they protrude from a bank, and trained into the desired shape; specimens of these hooks may be seen in almost any ethnographical museum. To sink the line, coral stones of three or four pounds weight are used, attached by a very thin piece of cinnet or bark, which, when the fish is struck, is always broken by its struggles, and falls off, thus releasing the line from an unnecessary weight. It is no light task hauling in a thick, heavy line, hanging straight up and down for a length of from seventy-five to a hundred fathoms or more!

Each canoe is manned by four men, only two of whom usually fish, the other two, one at the bow and the other at the stern, being employed in keeping the little craft in a stationary position with their paddles. If, however, there is not much current all four lower their lines, one man working his paddle with one hand so as to keep from drifting. My usual companions were the resident native teacher and two stalwart young natives of the island--Tulu'ao and Muli'ao; and I may here indulge in a little vanity when I say that my success as a *palu*-fisher was regarded as something phenomenal, only one other white man in the group, a trader on the atoll of Funafuti, having ever caught a *palu*, or, in fact, tried to catch one. But then I had such beautiful tackle that even the most skilled native fisherman had no chance when competing with me. My lines were of twenty-seven-strand white American cotton, as thick as a small goose-quill, and easily handled, never tangling or twisting like the native cinnet; and my hooks were the admiration and envy of all who saw them. They were of the "flatted" Kirby type, eyed, but with a curve in the shank, which was five inches in length, and as thick as a lead-pencil. I had bought these in Sydney, and during the voyage down had rigged them with snoodings of the very best seizing wire, intending to use them for shark-fishing. I had smaller ones down to three inches, but always preferred using the largest size, as the *palu* has a large mouth, and it is a difficult matter in a small canoe on a dark night to free a hook embedded in the gullet of a fish which is awkward to handle even when exhausted, and weighing as much as sixty or seventy pounds; while I also knew that any unusual noise or commotion would be almost sure to attract some of those most dangerous of all night-prowlers of the Pacific, the deep-water blue shark.

Paddling out due westward from the lee side of the island, where the one village is situated, we would bring-to in about seventy or eighty fathoms. As I always used leaden sinkers, my companions invariably let me lower first to test the depth, as with a two or three-pound lead my comparatively thin line took but little time in running out and touching bottom. A whole flying-fish was used for one bait by the natives, it being tied on to the inner curve of the great wooden hook, whilst I cut one in half, fore-and-aft, and ran my hook through it lengthwise.

The utmost silence was always observed; and even when lighting our pipes we were always careful not to let the reflection of the flame of the match fall upon the water, on account of the sharks, which would at once be attracted to the canoe, and hover about until they were rewarded for their vigilance by seizing the first *palu* brought to the surface. Sometimes a hungry shark will seize the outrigger in his jaws, or get foul of it, and upset the canoe, and a capsize under such circumstances is a serious matter indeed. For this reason the canoes are never far apart from each other; if one should be attacked or disabled by a shark the others at once render assistance, and the shark is usually thrust through with a lance if he is too big to be captured and killed. All haste is then made to get away from the spot, leaving the disturber of the proceedings to be devoured by his companions, whom the scent of blood soon brings upon the scene.

With ordinary luck we would get our first *palu* within an hour of lowering our lines. At such a great depth as eighty or ninety fathoms a bite would scarcely be felt by one of my companions on his thick, heavy, and clumsy line; but on mine it was very different, and there was hardly an occasion on which I did not secure the first fish. Like most bottom-haunting fish in very deep water the *palu* makes but a brief fight. If he can succeed in "getting his head," he will at once rush into the coral forest amid which he lives, and endeavour to save himself by jamming his body into a cleft or chasm of rock, and let the hook be torn from his jaws, which are soft, boneless, and glutinous. Once, however, he is dragged clear of the coral he seems to lose all heart; and, although he makes an occasional spurt, he grows weaker and weaker as he is dragged toward the surface, and when lifted into the canoe is apparently lifeless, his large eyes literally standing out of his head, and his stomach distended like a balloon. So enormous is the distention of the bladder that sometimes it will protrude from the mouth, and then burst with a noise like a pistol-shot! Perhaps some of my readers will smile at this, but they could see the same thing occur with other deep-sea fish besides the *palu*. In the Caroline and Marshall Islands there is a species of grey groper which is caught in a depth ranging from one hundred to one hundred and fifty fathoms; these fish, which range up to two hundred pounds, actually burst their stomachs when brought to the surface; for the air in the cavities of the body expands on the removal of the great pressure which at such depths keeps it compressed.

Now as to the appearance of the *palu*. When first caught, and seen by the light of a lantern or torch, it is a dark, silvery grey in colour, with prickly, inverted scales--like the feathers of a French fowl of a certain breed. The head is somewhat cod-shaped, with eyes quite as large as a crown-piece; the teeth are many, small, and soft, and bend to a firm pressure; and the bones in the fin and tail are so soft and flexible that they may be bent into any shape, but when dried are of the appearance and consistency of gelatine. The length of the largest *palu* I have seen was five feet six inches, with a girth of about forty inches. This one was caught in about ninety fathoms of water; and when I opened the stomach I found it to contain five or six undigested fish, about seven inches in length, of the groper species, and for which the natives of the island had no name or knowledge of beyond the appellation *ika kehe*--"unknown fish"--that is, fish which are only seen when taken from the stomach of a deep-sea fish, or are brought to the surface or washed ashore after some submarine disturbance.

The flesh of the *palu* is greatly valued by the natives of the equatorial islands of the Pacific for its medicinal qualities as a laxative, whilst the oil with which it is permeated is much used as a remedy for rheumatism and similar complaints. Within half an hour of its being taken from the water the skin changes to a dead black, and the flesh assumes the appearance of whale blubber. Generally, the fish is cooked in the usual native ground-oven as quickly as possible, care being taken to wrap it closely up in the broad leaves of the *puraka* plant--a species of gigantic taro--in order that none of the oil may be lost. Thinking that the oil, which is perfectly colourless and with scarcely any odour, might prove of value, I once "tried out" two of the largest fish taken, and obtained a gallon. This I sent to a firm of drug-merchants in Sydney; but unfortunately the vessel was lost on the passage.

The *palu* does not seem to have a wide habitat. In the Tonga Islands it is, I believe, very rare; and in Fiji, Samoa, and other mountainous groups throughout Polynesia the natives appear to have no knowledge of it, although they have a fish possessing the same peculiar characteristics, but of a somewhat different shape. I have fished for it without success at half a dozen places in Samoa, in New Britain, and New Ireland. But it is generally to be found about the coasts of any of the low-lying coral islands of the Union (or Tokelau) Group, the Ellice, Gilbert, Marshall, and part of the Caroline archipelagoes. The Gilbert Islanders call it *te ika ne peka*--a name that cannot well be translated into bald English, though there is a very lucid Latin equivalent.

In 1882 I took passage from the Island of Nukufetau in the Ellice Group for the Caroline Islands. The vessel was a fine brigantine of 160 tons, and was named the *Orwell*. She was, unfortunately, commanded by an incompetent, obstinate, self-willed man, who, though a good seaman, had no meteorological knowledge and succeeded in losing the ship, when lying at anchor, on Peru Island, in the Gilbert Group, ten days after leaving Nukufetau, simply through disregarding the local trader's advice to put to sea. Disastrous as was the incident to me, for I lost trade goods and personal effects to the value of over a thousand pounds, and came ashore with what I stood in--to wit, a pyjama suit--and a bag of Chili dollars, I had reason to afterwards congratulate myself from a fisherman's point of view.

Living on the island was a Swiss, Frank Voliero, whom I have before mentioned. He was an ardent deep-sea fisherman, and was on that account highly respected by the natives, who otherwise did not care for him, as he was of an exceedingly quarrelsome disposition. He was an expert *palu* man, and he and I therefore quickly made Island *bruderschaft*. During the three months I remained on Peru we had many fishing trips, and caught not less than fifty *palu*. The largest of these was evidently a patriarch, for although he was in rather poor condition he weighed 136 lbs. and was 6 feet 10 inches in length. Another, hooked at a depth of eighty-five fathoms, was only 5 feet 2 inches, and weighed 129 lbs. Its stomach contained a small octopus with curiously stunted tentacles, almost as thick at the tips as they were at the base, but in all other respects similar to those found in shallow water upon the reefs and in the lagoon.

Both Voliero and myself tried many kinds of bait for *palu,* believing that the native theory that the fish would only take flying-fish was wrong. We found that on Peru, any elongated fish, such as gars, silvery mullet, or young bonito, were acceptable, and that the tentacle of an octopus, after the outer skin was removed, answered just as well. Yet further southward among the Pacific Isles, flying-fish is the only bait they will take! Evidently, therefore, the *palu*, at the great depths in which it lives, is attracted by a brightly-hued fish whose habitat is on the surface of the ocean. Why this is so must be decided by ichthyologists, for there are no bright, silvery-scaled fish inhabiting the ocean at such depths as eighty or a hundred fathoms. And why is it that the *palu,* quiescent by day, and feeding only at night, so eagerly seizes a hook baited with a flying-fish--a fish which never descends more than a few fathoms below the surface, and which the *palu* can never possibly see except when it is lowered by human hands to, or sinks to the bottom?

Of the marvellous efficacy of the *palu*-oil in a case of acute rheumatism I can speak with knowledge. The second mate of an island-trading schooner of which I was the supercargo, was landed at Arorai, in the Line Islands, unable to move, and suffering great agony. After two days' massaging with *palu*-oil he recovered and returned to his duties.

[Since this was written I have learned that Mr. E.R. Waite, of the Sydney Museum, has described the *palu* as the ***Ruvettus pretiosus***, "which hitherto was known only from the North Atlantic, and whose recorded range is now enormously increased. The Escolar--to give it its Atlantic name--has been taken at depths as great as three and four hundred fathoms, but can only be taken at night in September and the early part of October." I should very much like to learn how the *palu* is taken at a depth of four hundred fathoms--eight hundred yards!]

The Wily "Goanner"

In the early part of the year 1899 a settler named Hardy, residing at Glenowlan, in the Rylstone district of New South Wales, about 150 miles from Sydney, lost numbers of his lambs during the lambing season. Naturally enough, dingoes were suspected, but none were seen. Then other sheep--men began to lose lambs, and a close watch was set, with the result that iguanas, which are very numerous in this part of the country, were discovered to be the murderers of the little "baa-baa's." The cause of this new departure in the predatory habits of the "goanner"--which hitherto had confined his evil deeds to nocturnal visits to the fowl-yards--is stated to be the extermination of the opossum, which has driven the cunning reptile to seek for another source of food. And, as before the shooting of kangaroos, wallabies, and opossums was resorted to as a means of livelihood by hundreds of bushmen who had no other employment open to them, the young of these marsupials furnished the iguana with an ample supply of food, the theory is very probably correct. Poison will be the only method of destroying or reducing the numbers of the iguana, who, robber as he is, yet has his good points, as has even the sneaking, blood-loving native cat--for both are merciless foes to snakes of all kinds; and 'tis better to have an energetic and hungry native cat and a score of wily iguanas working havoc among the tenants of your fowl-house than one brown or an equally deadly "bandy-bandy" snake within half a mile.

In that part of New South Wales in which the writer was born--one of the tidal rivers on the northern coast--both snakes and iguanas were plentiful, and a source of continual worry to the settlers.

On one occasion some boyish companions and myself set to work to build a raft for fishing purposes out of some old and discarded blue gum rails which were lying along the bank of the river. Boy-like, we utterly disregarded our parents' admonition to put on our boots, and, aided by a couple of blackfellows, we moved about the long grass on our bare feet, picking up the heavy rails and carrying them on our shoulders, one by one, down to the sandy beach, where we were to lash them together. Presently we came across a very heavy rail, about eight feet long, twelve inches in width, and two inches thick. It was no sooner up-ended than we saw half a dozen "bandy-bandies"--the smallest but most deadly of Australian snakes, not even excepting the death-adder--lying beneath! We gave a united yell of terror and fled as the black and yellow banded reptiles--none of which were over eighteen inches in length nor thicker than a man's little finger--wriggled between our feet into the long grass around us. For some minutes we were too frightened at our escape to speak; but soon set to work to complete the raft. Presently one of the blackfellows pointed to a tall honeysuckle-tree about fifty feet away, and said with a gleeful chuckle, "Hallo, you see him that 'pfeller goanner been catch him bandy-bandy?"

Sure enough, an iguana, about three feet in length, was scurrying up the rough, ridgy bark of the honeysuckle with a "bandy-bandy" in his jaws. He had seized the snake by its head, I imagine, for we could see the rest of its form twisting and turning about and enveloping the body of its capturer. In a few seconds we saw the iguana ascend still higher, then he disappeared with his hateful prey among the loftier branches. No doubt he enjoyed his meal.

About a year or so later I was given another instance of the "cuteness" of the wicked "goanner." My sister (aged twelve) and myself (two years younger) were fishing with bamboo rods for mullet. We were standing, one on each side, of the rocky edges of a tiny little bay on the coast near Port Macquarie (New South Wales). The background was a short, steep beach of soft, snow-white sand, fringed at the high-water margin with a dense jungle of wild apple and pandanus-trees.

The mullet bit freely, and as we swung the gleaming, bright-silvered fish out of the water on to the rocks on which we stood, we threw them up on to the beach, and left them to kick about and coat themselves with the clean, white sand--which they did in such an artistic manner that one would imagine they considered it egg and breadcrumb, and were preparing themselves to fulfil their ultimate and proper use to the *genus homo*.

My sister had caught seven and I five, when, the sun being amidships, we decided to boil the billy of tea and get something to eat; young mullet, roasted on a glowing fire of honeysuckle cobs were, we knew, very nice. So, laying down our rods on the rocks, we walked up to the beach--just in time to see two "goanners"-- one of them with a wriggling mullet in his mouth--scamper off into the bush.

A careful search revealed the harrowing fact that nine of the twelve fish were missing, and the multitudinous criss-cross tracks on the sand showed the cause of their disappearance. My sister sat down on a hollow log and wept, out of sheer vexation of spirit, while I lit a fire to boil the billy and grill the three remaining mullet. Then after we had eaten the fish and drank some tea, we concocted a plan of deadly revenge. We took four large bream-hooks, bent them on to a piece of fishing-line, baited each hook with a good-sized piece of octopus (our mullet bait), and suspended the line between two saplings, about three inches above the leaf-strewn ground. Then, feeling confident of the success of our murderous device, we finished the billy of tea and went back to our fishing. We caught a couple of dozen or more of fine mullet, each one weighing not less than 1-1/2 lbs.; and then the incoming tide with its sweeping seas drove us from the ledge of rocks to the beach, where we changed our bamboo rods for hand-lines with sinkers, and flung them, baited with chunks of mullet, out into the breaking surf for sea-bream. By four in the afternoon we had caught more fish than we could well carry home, five miles away; and after stringing the mullet and bream through the gills with a strip of supple-jack cane, we went up the beach to our camp for the billy can and basket.

And then we saw a sight that struck terror into our guilty souls--a ***Danse Macabre*** of three writhing black and yellow, long-tailed "goanners," twisting, turning and lashing their sinuous and scaly tails in agony as they sought to free their widely-opened jaws from the cruel hooks. One had two hooks in his mouth. He was the quietest of the lot, as he had less purchase than the other two upon the ground, and with one hook in his lower and one in his upper jaw, glared upwards at us in his torture and smote his sides with his long, thin tail.

"Oh, you wicked, wicked boy!" said my partner in guilt--at once shifting the responsibility of the whole affair upon me--"you ought to be ashamed of yourself for doing such a thing! You know well enough that we should never hurt a poor, harmless iguana. Oh, *do* take those horrible hooks out of the poor things' mouths and let them go, you wicked, cruel boy!"

With my heart in my mouth I crept round through the scrub, knife in hand.

"Go on, you horrible, horrible, coward!" screamed my sister; "one would think that the poor things were alligators or sharks. Oh, my goodness, if you're so frightened, I'll come and do it myself." With that she clambered up into the branches of a pandanus-tree and looked at me excitedly, mingled with considerable contempt and much fear.

Being quite wise enough not to attempt to take the hooks out of the "goanners'" mouths, I cut the two ends of the line to which they hung. They instantly sought refuge on the tree trunks around them; but as each "goanner" selected his individual tree, and as they were still connected to each other by the line and the hooks in their jaws, their attempts to reach a higher plane was a failure. So they fell to upon one another savagely.

"Come away, you wicked, thoughtless boy," said my sister, weepingly. "I shall never come out with you again; you cruel thing."

Then, overcoming my fear, I valiantly advanced, and gingerly extending my arm, cut the tangled-up fishing line in a dozen places; and with my bamboo fishing-rod disintegrated the combatants. They stood for a few seconds, panting and open-mouthed, and then, with the hooks still fast in their jaws, scurried away into the scrub.

The Ta~nifa of Samoa

Many years ago, at the close of an intensely hot day, I set out from Apia, the principal port of Samoa, to walk to a village named Laulii, a few miles along the coast. Passing through the semi-Europeanised town of Matautu, I emerged out upon the open beach. I was bound on a pigeon-shooting trip to the mountains, but intended sleeping that night at Laulii with some native friends who were to accompany me. With me was a young Manhiki half-caste named Allan Strickland; he was about twenty-two years of age and one of the most perfect specimens of athletic manhood in the South Pacific.[15] For six months we had been business partners and comrades in a small cutter in which we traded between Apia and Sava'ii--the largest island of the Samoan group; and now after some months of toil we were taking a week's holiday together, and enjoying ourselves greatly, although at the time (1873) the country was in the throes of an internecine war.

A walk of a mile brought us to the mouth of the Vaivasa River, a small stream flowing into the sea from the littoral on our right. The tide was high and we therefore hailed a picket who were stationed in the trenches on the opposite bank and asked them in a jocular manner not to fire at us while we were wading across. To our surprise, for we were both well known to and on very friendly terms with the contending parties, half a dozen of them sprang up and excitedly bade us not to attempt to cross.

"Go further up the bank and cross to our *olo* (lines) in a canoe," added a young Manono chief whose family I knew well, "there is a ta~nifa about. We saw it last night."

That was quite enough for us--for the name Ta~nifa sent a cold chill down our backs. We turned to the right, and after walking a quarter of a mile came to a hut on the bank at a spot regarded as neutral ground. Here we found some women and children and a canoe, and in less than five minutes we were landed on the other side, the women chorusing the dreadful fate that would have befallen us had we attempted to cross at the mouth of the river.

"*E lima gafa le umi!*" ("'Tis five fathoms long!") cried one old dame.

"And a fathom wide at the shoulders," said another bare-bosomed lady, with a shudder. "It hath come to the mouth of the Vaivasa because it hath smelt the blood of the three men who were killed in the river here two days ago."

"We'll hear the true yarn presently," said my companion as we walked down the left-hand bank of the river. "There must be a ta˜nifa cruising about, or else those Manono fellows wouldn't have been so scared at us wanting to cross."

As soon as we reached the young chief's quarters, we were made very welcome, and were obliged to accept his invitation to remain and share supper with himself and his men--all stalwart young natives from the little island of Manono--a lovely spot situated in the straits separating Upolo from Savaii. Placing our guns and bags in the care of one of the warriors, we took our seats on the matted floor, filled our pipes anew, and, whilst a bowl of kava was being prepared, Li'o, the young chief told us about the advent of the ta˜nifa.

Let me first of all, however, explain that the ta˜nifa is a somewhat rare and greatly-dreaded member of the old-established shark family. By many white residents in Samoa it was believed to occasionally reach a length of from twenty to twenty-five feet; as a matter of fact it seldom exceeds ten feet, but its great girth, and its solitary, nocturnal habit of haunting the mouths of shallow streams has invested it even to the native mind with fictional powers of voracity and destruction. Yet, despite the exaggerated accounts of the creature, it is really a dreadful monster, rendered the more dangerous to human life by the persistency with which it frequents muddied and shallow water, particularly after a freshet caused by heavy rain, when its presence cannot be discerned.

Into the port of Apia there fall two small streams--called "rivers" by the local people--the Mulivai and the Vaisigago, and I was fortunate to see specimens of the ta˜nifa **on three occasions, twice at the Vaisigago, and once at the mouth of the Mulivai, but I had never seen one caught, or even sufficiently exposed to give me an idea of its proportions. Many natives, however--particularly an old**

Rarotongan named Hapai, who lived in Apia, and was the proud capturer of several ta~nifa--gave me a reliable description, which I afterwards verified.

A ta~nifa ten feet long, they assured me, was an enormously bulky and powerful creature with jaws and teeth much larger than an ocean-haunting shark of double that length; the width across the shoulders was very great, and although it generally swam slowly, it would, when it had once sighted its prey, dart along under the water with great rapidity without causing a ripple. At a village in Savaii, a powerfully built woman who was incautiously bathing at the mouth of a stream was seized by one of these sharks almost before she could utter a cry, so swiftly and suddenly was she attacked. Several attempts were made to capture the brute, which continued to haunt the scene of the tragedy for several days, but it was too cunning to take a hook and was never caught.

This particular ta~nifa*, which had been seen by the young Manono chief and his men on the preceding evening had made its appearance soon after darkness had fallen and had cruised to and fro across the mouth of the Vaivasa till the tide began to fall, when it made its way seaward through a passage in the reef. It was, so Li'o assured me, quite eight feet in length and very wide across the head and shoulders. The water was clear and by the bright starlight they had discerned its movements very easily; once it came well into the river and remained stationary for some minutes, lying under about two feet of water. Some of the Manono men, hailing a picket of the enemy on the opposite bank of the river, asked for a ten minutes' truce to try and shoot it; this was granted, and standing on top of the sandy trench, half a dozen young fellows fired a volley at the shark from their Sniders. None of the bullets took effect and the* ta~nifa sailed slowly off again to cruise to and fro for another hour, watching for any hapless person who might cross the river.

Just as the kava was being handed round, some children who were on watch cried out that the ta~nifa *had come. Springing to his feet, Li'o again hailed the enemy's picket on the other side, and a truce was agreed to, so that "the white men could have a look at the* ma|lie"--shark.

Thirty or forty yards away was what seemed to be a huge, irregular and waving mass of phosphorus which, as it drew nearer, revealed the outlines of the dreaded fish. It came in straight for the mouth of the creek, passed over the pebbly bar, and then swam leisurely about in the brackish water, moving from bank to bank at less than a dozen feet from the shore. The stream of bright phosphorescent light which had surrounded its body when it first appeared had now, owing to there being but a minor degree of phosphorus in the brackish water, given place to a dulled, sickly, greenish reflection, accentuated however by thin, vivid streaks, caused by the exudation from the gills of a streaming, viscid matter, common to some species of sharks, and giving it a truly terrifying and horrible appearance. Presently a couple of natives, taking careful aim, fired at the creature's head; in an instant it darted off with extraordinary velocity, rushing through the water like a submerged comet--if I may use the illustration. Both of the men who had fired were confident their bullets had struck and badly wounded the shark, but were greatly disgusted when, ten minutes later, it again appeared, swimming leisurely about, at ten fathoms from the beach.

Three days later, as we were returning to Apia, we were told by our native friends that the shark still haunted the mouth of the Vaivasa; and I determined to capture it. I sent Allan on board the cutter for our one shark hook--a hook which had done much execution among the sea prowlers. Although not of the largest size, being only ten inches in the shank, it was made of splendid steel, and we had frequently caught fifteen-feet sharks with it at sea. It was a cherished possession with us and we always kept it--and the four feet of chain to which it was attached--bright and clean.

In the evening Allan returned, accompanied by the local pilot (a Captain Hamilton) and the fat, puffing, master of a German barque. They wanted "to see the fun." We soon had everything in readiness; the hook, baited with the belly-portion of a freshly-killed pig (which the Manono people had commandeered from a bush village) was buoyed to piece of light *pua* wood to keep it from sinking, and then with twenty fathoms of brand-new whale line attached, we let it drift out into the centre of the passage. Then making our end of the line fast to the trunk of a coconut tree, we set some children to watch, and went into the trenches to drink some kava, smoke, and gossip.

We had not long to wait--barely half an hour--when we heard a warning yell from the watchers. The ta~nifa was in sight.

Jumping up and tumbling over each other in our eagerness we rushed out; but alas! too late for the shark; for instead of approaching in its usual leisurely manner, it made a straight dart at the bait, and before we could free our end of the line it was as taut as an iron bar, and the creature, with the hook firmly fastened in his jaw, was ploughing the water into foam, amid yells of excitement from the natives. Then suddenly the line fell slack, and the half-a-dozen men who were holding it went over on their backs, heels up.

In mournful silence we hauled it in, and then, oh woe! the hook, our prized, our beautiful hook, was gone! and with it two feet of the chain, which had parted at the centre swivel. That particular ta˜nifa was seen no more.

Nearly two months later, two ta˜nifa *of a much larger size, appeared at the mouth of the Vaivasa. Several of the white residents tried, night after night, to hook them, but the monsters refused to look at the baits. Then appeared on the scene an old one-eyed Malay named 'Reo, who asserted he could kill them easily. The way in which he set to work was described to me by the natives who witnessed the operations. Taking a piece of green bamboo, about four feet in length, he split from it two strips each an inch wide. The ends of these he then, after charring the points, sharpened carefully; then by great pressure he coiled them up into as small a compass as possible, keeping the whole in position by sewing the coil up in the fresh skin of a fish known as the* isuumu moana--a species of the "leather-jacket." Then he asked to be provided with two dogs. A couple of curs were soon provided, killed, and the viscera removed. The coils of bamboo were then placed in the vacancy and the skin of the bellies stitched up with small wooden skewers. That completed the preparation of the baits.

As soon as the two sharks made their appearance, one of the dead dogs was thrown into the water. It was quickly swallowed. Then the second followed, and was also seized by the other ta˜nifa. The creatures cruised about for some hours, then went off, as the tide began to fall.

On the following evening they did not turn up, nor on the next; but the Malay insisted that within four or five days both would be dead. As soon as the dogs were digested, he said, the thin fish-skin would follow, the bamboo coil would fly apart, and the sharpened ends penetrate not only the sharks' intestines, but protrude through the outer skin as well.

Quite a week afterwards, during which time neither of the ta~nifa had been seen alive, the smaller of the two was found dead on the beach at Vailele Plantation, about four miles from the Vaivasa. It was examined by numbers of people, and presented an extremely interesting sight; one end of the bamboo spring was protruding over a foot from the belly, which was so cut and lacerated by the agonised efforts of the monster to free itself from the instrument of torture, that much of the intestines was gone.

That the larger of these dreaded fish had died in the same manner there was no reason to doubt; but probably it had sunk in the deep water outside the barrier reef.

On Board the "Tucopia."

The little island trading barque *Tucopia*, Henry Robertson, master, lay just below Garden Island in Sydney Harbour, ready to sail for the Friendly Islands and Samoa as soon as the captain came on board. At nine o'clock, as Bruce, the old, white-haired, Scotch mate, was pointing out to Mrs. Lacy and the Reverend Wilfrid Lacy the many ships around, and telling them from whence they came or where they were bound, the second mate called out--

"Here's the captain's boat coming, sir."

Bruce touched his cap to the pale-faced, violet-eyed clergyman's wife, and turning to the break of the poop, at once gave orders to "heave short," leaving the field clear to Mr. Charles Otway, the supercargo of the *Tucopia*, who was twenty-two years of age, had had seven years' experience of general wickedness in the South Seas, thought he was in love with Mrs. Lacy, and that, before the barque reached Samoa, he would make the lady feel that the Reverend Wilfrid was a serious mistake, and that he, Charles Otway, was the one man in the world whom she could love and be happy with for ever. So, being a hot-blooded and irresponsible young villain, though careful and decorous to all outward seeming, he set himself to work, took exceeding care over his yellow, curly hair, and moustache, and abstained from swearing in Mrs. Lacy's hearing.

*　　*　　*　　*　　*

A week before, Mr. and Mrs. Lacy had called at the owner's office and inquired about a passage to Samoa in the *Tucopia*, and Otway was sent for.

"Otway," said the junior partner, "can you make room on the *Tucopia* for two more passengers--nice people, a clergyman and his wife."

"D----all nice people, especially clergymen and their wives," he answered promptly--for although the youngest supercargo in the firm, he was considered, the smartest--and took every advantage of the fact. "I'm sick of carting these confounded missionaries about, Mr. Harry. Last trip we took two down to Tonga--beastly hymn-grinding pair, who wanted the hands to come aft every night to prayers, and played-up generally with the discipline of the ship. Robertson never interfered, and old Bruce, who is one of the psalm-singing kidney himself, encouraged the beasts to turn the ship into a floating Bethel."

"Mr. Harry" laughed good-naturedly. "Otway, my boy, you mustn't put on so much side--the firm can't afford it. If you hadn't drunk so much whisky last night you would be in a better temper this morning."

"Oh, if you've got some one else to take my billet on the *Tucopia*, why don't you say so, instead of backing and filling about, like a billy-goat in stays? *I* don't care a damn if you load the schooner up to her maintop with sky-pilots and their dowdy women-kind. I've had enough of 'em, and I hereby tender you my resignation. I can get another and a better ship to-morrow, if--"

"Sit down, you cock-a-hoopy young ass," and "Mr. Harry" hit the supercargo a good-humoured but stiff blow in the chest. "These people aren't missionaries; they're a cut above the usual breed. Man's a gentleman; woman's as sweet as a rosebud. Now look here, Otway; we give you a pretty free hand generally, but in this instance we want you to stretch a point--you can give these people berths in the trade-room, can't you?"

The supercargo considered a moment. "There's a lot returning this trip. First, there's the French priest for Wallis Island--nice old buffer, but never washes, and grinds his teeth in his sleep--he's in the cabin next to mine; old Miss Wiedermann for Tonga--cabin on starboard side--fussy old cat, who is always telling me that she can distinctly hear Robertson's bad language on deck. But her brother is a good sort, and so I put up with her. Then there's Captain Burr, in the skipper's cabin, two Samoan half-caste girls in the deck-house--there's going to be trouble over those women, old Bruce says, and I don't doubt it--and the whole lot will have their meals in the beastly dog-kennel you call a saloon, and I call a sweat-box."

"Thank you, Mr. Otway. Your elegant manner of speaking shows clearly the refining influence of the charming people with whom you associate. Just let me tell you this--you looked like a gentleman a year or two ago, but become less like one every day."

"No wonder," replied Otway sullenly, "the Island trade is not calculated to turn out Chesterfields. I'm sick enough of it, now we are carrying passengers as well as cargo. I suppose the firm will be asking us supercargoes to wear uniform and brass buttons soon, like the ticket collector on a penny ferry."

"Quite likely, my sulky young friend--quite likely, if it will pay us to do so."

"Then I'll clear out, and go nigger-catching again in the Solomons. That's a lot better than having to be civil to people who worry the soul out of you, are always in the way at sea, and a beastly nuisance in port. Why, do you know what old Miss Weidermann did at Manono, in Samoa, when we were there buying yams three months ago?"

"No; what did she do?"

"Got the skipper and myself into a howling mess through her infernal interference; and if the chiefs and old Mataafa himself had not come to our help there would have been some shooting, and this firm could never have sent another ship to Manono again. It makes me mad when I think of it--the silly old bundle of propriety and feminine spite."

"Tell me all about it, Otway. 'Twill do you good, I can see, to unburden yourself of some of your bad temper. Shut that door, and we'll have a brandy-and-soda together."

"Well," said Otway, "this is what occurred. I was ashore in the village, buying and weighing the yams, the skipper was lending me a hand, and everything was going on bully, when Mataafa and his chiefs sent an invitation to us to come up to his house and drink kava. Of course such an invitation from the native point of view was a great honour; and then, besides that, it was good business to keep in with old Mataafa, who had just given the Germans a thrashing at Vailele, and was as proud as a dog with two tails. So, although I hate kava, I accepted the invitation with 'many expressions of pleasure,' and felt sure that as the old fellow knew me of old, and I knew he wanted to buy some rifles, that I should get the bulk of a bag of sovereigns his mongrel, low-down American secretary was carrying around. So oft went the skipper and I, letting the yams stand over till we returned; the barque was lying about a mile off the beach. Mataafa was very polite to us, and during the kava drinking I found out that he had about three hundred sovereigns, and wanted to see the Martini-Henrys we had on board. Of course I told him that it would be a serious business for the ship if he gave us away--imprisonment in a dreadful dungeon in Fiji, if not hanging at the yard-arm or a man-of-war--and the old cock winked his eye and laughed. Then, as time was valuable, we at once concocted a plan to get the rifles--fifty--ashore without making too much of a show. Well, among some of the women present there were two great swells, one was the *taupo*, or town maid, of Palaulae in Savaii, and the other was a niece of Mataafa himself. These two, accompanied by a lot of young women of Manono, were to go off on board the barque in our boats, ostensibly to pay their respects to the white lady on board, and invite her on shore, so as to get her out of the way; then I was to pass the arms out of the stern ports into some canoes which would be waiting just as it became dark. About five o'clock they started off in one boat, leaving me and the skipper to follow in another. I had sent a note off to the mate telling him all about the little game, and to be mighty polite to the two chief women, who were to be introduced to Miss Weidermann, give the old devil some presents of mats, fruits, and such things, and ask her to come ashore as Mataafa's guest.

"Well, something had gone wrong with the Weidermann's temper; for when the women came on board she was sulking in her cabin, and refused to show her vinegary face outside her state-room door. Thinking she would get over her tantrum in a few minutes, the mate invited the two Samoan ladies and their attendants down into the cabin, where they awaited her appearance, behaving themselves, of course, very decorously, it being a visit of ceremony.

"Presently Old Cat-face opened her door, and then, without giving the native ladies time to utter a word, she launched out at them in her bastard-mongrel Samoan-Tongan. The first thing she said was that she knew the kind of women they were, and what had brought them on board! How dared such brazen, shameless cattle come into the cabin! Into the same cabin as a white lady! The bold, half-naked, disgraceful hussies, etc., etc. And then she capped the thing by calling to the steward to come and drive them out!

"Not one of the native women could answer her. They were all simply dumbfounded at such a gross insult, and left the cabin in silence. The mate tried to smooth things over, but one of the women--Mataafa's niece--gave him a look that told him to say no more. In half an hour the whole lot of them were back on the beach, and came up to the chiefs house, where the skipper and myself were having a final drink of kava with old Mataafa and his *faipule*.[16] The face of the elder of the two women was blazing with anger, and then, pointing to the captain and myself, she gave us such a tongue-lashing for sending her off to the ship to be shamed and insulted, that made us blush. Old Mataafa waited until she had finished, and then, with an ugly gleam in his eye but speaking very quietly, asked us what it meant.

"What *could* we say but that it was no fault of ours; and then, by a happy inspiration, I added that although Miss Weidermann was generally well-conducted enough, she sometimes got blazing drunk, and made a beast of herself. This explanation satisfied the chiefs, if not the women, and everything went on smoothly. And as it was then nearly dark, and I was determined that Mataafa should get his rifles, half a dozen of his men took us off in their canoes, and we went on board. The skipper and I had fixed up as to what we should do with the Weidermann creature. She was seated at the cabin table waiting to open out on us, but the skipper didn't give her a chance.

"'Go to your cabin at once, madam,' he said solemnly, 'and I trust you will not again leave it in your present condition. Your conduct is simply astounding. *Steward, see that you give Miss Weidermann no more grog*.'

"The poor old girl thought that either he or she herself was going mad, but he gave her no time to talk. The captain opened her state-room door, gently pushed her in, and put a man outside to see that she didn't come out again. Then we handed out the rifles through the stern-ports to the natives in the canoes, and sent them away rejoicing. And that's the end of the yarn, and Miss Weidermann nearly went into a fit next morning when we told her that no less than thirty respectable native women had taken their oaths that she was mad drunk, and abused them vilely."

The junior partner laughed loudly at the story, and Otway, with a more amiable look on his face, rose.

"Well, I'll do what I can for these people. I'll make room for them somehow. Where are they going?"

"Samoa. They have an idea of settling down there, I think, for a few months, and then going on to China. They have plenty of money, apparently."

"Oh, well, tell them to come on board to-morrow, and I'll show them what can be done for them."

*   *   *   *   *

So the Rev. and Mrs. Lacy did come on board, and Mr. Charles Otway was vanquished by just one single glance from the lady's violet eyes.

"It would have been such a dreadful disappointment to us if we could not have obtained passages in the *Tucopia*," she said, in her soft, sweet voice, as she sank back in the deck-chair he placed before her. "My husband is so bent on making a tour through Samoa. Now, do tell me, Mr. Otway, are these islands so very lovely?"

"Very, very lovely, Mrs. Lacy," replied Otway, leaning with his back against the rail and regarding her with half-closed eyes; "as sweet and fair to look upon as a lovely woman--a woman with violet eyes and lips like a budding rose."

She gave him one swift glance, seemingly in anger, yet her eyes smiled into his; then she bent her head and regarded the deck with intense interest. Otway thought he had scored. She was sure *she* had.

Otway had just shown her and her husband his own cabin, and had told them that they could occupy it--he would make himself comfortable in the trade-room, he said. This was after the first look from the violet eyes.

*   *   *   *   *

Robertson, the skipper, came aboard, shook hands with Mrs. Lacy and her husband, nodded to the other passengers, dived below for a moment or two, and then reappeared on deck, full of energy, blasphemy, and anxiety to get under way. In less than an hour the smart barque was outside the Heads, and heeling over to a brisk south-westerly breeze. Two days later she was four hundred miles on her course.

The Rev. Wilfrid Lacy soon made himself very agreeable to the rest of the passengers, who all agreed that he was a splendid type of parson, and even Otway, who had as much principle as a rat and began making love to his wife from the outset, liked him. First of all, he was not the usual style of travelling clergyman. He didn't say grace at meals, he smoked a pipe, drank whisky and brandy with Otway and Robertson, told rattling good stories, and displayed an immediate interest when the skipper mentioned that the second mate was a "bit of a bruiser," and that there were gloves on board; and the second mate, a nuggety little Tynesider, at once consented to a friendly mill as soon as he was off duty.

"Wilfrid," said Mrs. Lacy, "you'll shock every one. I can see that Captain Robertson wonders what sort of a clergyman you are."

Robertson saw the merry light in her dark eyes, and then laughed aloud as he saw Miss Weidermann's face. It expressed the very strongest disapproval, and during the rest of the meal the virgin lady preserved a dismal silence. The rest of the passengers, however, "took" to the clerical gentleman at once. With old Father Roget--the Marist missionary who sat opposite him--he soon entered into an animated conversation, while the two De Boos girls, vivacious Samoan half-castes, attached themselves to his wife. Seated beside Otway was another passenger, an American skipper named Burr, who was going to Apia to take command of a vessel belonging to the same firm as the *Tucopia*. He was a silent, good-looking man of about sixty, and possessed of much caustic humour and a remarkable fund of smoking-room stories, which, on rare occasions, he would relate in an inimitable, drawling manner, as if he was tired. The chief mate was a deeply but not obtrusively religious Scotsman; the second officer, Allen, was a young man of thirty, an excellent seaman, but rough to the verge of brutality with the crew. Bruce, on the other hand, was too easy-going and patient.

"I never want to raise my hand against a man," he said one day, as a protest, when Allen gave one of the crew an unmerciful cuff which sent him down as if he had been shot.

"Neither do I," replied Allen, "I prefer raising my foot. But it's habit, Mr. Bruce, only habit."

For five days the barque ran steadily on an E.N.E. course, then on the sixth day the wind hauled, and by sunset it was blowing hard from the eastward with a fast-gathering sea. By two in the morning Robertson and his officers knew that they were in for a three-days' easterly gale; a few hours later it was decided to heave-to, as the sea had become dangerous, and the little vessel was straining badly. Just after this had been done, the gale set in with redoubled fury, and when Mrs. Lacy came on deck shortly before breakfast, she shuddered at the wild spectacle. Coming to the break of the poop, she clasped the iron rail with both hands, and gazed fearfully about her.

"You had better go below, ma'am," said the second mate, who was standing near, talking to Otway, "there's some nasty, lumpy seas."

Then he gave a yell.

"Look out there!"

Springing to Mrs. Lacy's side, he clasped his left arm around her waist, and held on tightly to the iron rail with his right, just as a vast mountain of water took the barque amidships, fell on her deck with terrific force, and fairly buried her from the topgallant foc'scle to the level of the poop. In less than half a minute the galley, for'ard deck-house, long-boat, which was lying on the main hatch, and the port bulwarks had vanished, together with three poor seamen who were asleep in the deck-house. The fearful crash brought the captain flying on deck. One glance showed him that there was no chance of saving the men--to attempt to lower a boat in such a sea was utterly impossible, and would be madness itself. He sighed, and then took off his cap. Allen and Otway followed his example.

"Is there no hope for them?" Mrs. Lacy whispered to Otway.

"None," replied the supercargo in a low voice. "None." Then he urged her to go below, as it was not safe for her to remain on deck. She went at once, and met her husband just as he was leaving their cabin.

"What is the matter, Nell?" he asked, as he saw that tears were in her eyes.

"Three poor men have been carried overboard, Wilfrid. They were in the deck-house asleep ten minutes ago--now they are gone! Oh, isn't it dreadful, dreadful!" And then she sat down beside him and wept silently.

Breakfast was a forlorn meal--Robertson and his officers were not present, and Otway took the captain's seat. He, too, only remained to drink a cup of coffee, then hurriedly went on deck. Lacy rose at the same time, but at the foot of the companion, Otway motioned him to stop.

"Don't come on deck awhile, if you please," he said, "and tell the ladies to keep to the cabin."

"Anything fresh gone wrong?"

"Yes," replied the supercargo, looking steadily at the clergyman--"the ship is making water badly. Don't you hear the pumps going? Tell the ladies not to come on deck--say it is not safe. And if the old Weidermann girl hears the pumps, and gets inquisitive, tell her that a lot of water got into the hold when that big sea tumbled aboard. She's an inquisitive old ass, and would be bound to tell the other ladies that the ship is in danger."

Lacy nodded. "All right, I'll see to her. How long has the ship been leaking?"

"For quite a long time. And there is fourteen inches in her, and it's as much as we can do to keep it under."

"That is serious."

Otway nodded. "Yes, it is serious in weather like this. Now I must go. Daresay we may give you a call in the course of the morning. Ever try a spell at old-fashioned brake pumps? Fine exercise."

"I'm ready now if you want me," was the quiet answer.

The *Tucopia* was indeed in a pretty bad case. Immediately after the fatal sea had swept her decks the carpenter had sounded the well and found fifteen inches of water, some little of which had got below through the fore-scuttle, but the greater portion, it was soon evident, was the result of a leak. The barque was a comparatively new vessel, and Robertson and his officers, after two hours' pumping, came to the conclusion that she had either strained herself badly or a butt-end had started somewhere.

For two hours the crew worked at the pumps, taking a spell of ten minutes every half-hour, Otway, the American captain Burr, and Mr. Lacy all lending a hand. Then the well was sounded, and showed two inches less.

Robertson ordered the men to come aft and get a glass of grog. They trooped down into the cabin wet and exhausted, and the steward served them each out half a tumblerful of good French brandy. They drank it off, and then went on deck again to have a smoke before resuming pumping. A quarter of an hour later the pumps choked. There were a hundred tons of coal in the lower hold, and some of the small of it had been drawn up. By the time the carpenter had them cleared the water had gained seven inches, and the little barque was labouring heavily. Again, however, the willing crew turned to and pumped steadily for another hour, but only succeeded in reducing the water by an inch or two. Then Robertson called his officers together and consulted.

"We can't keep on like this much longer," he said, "the water is gaining on us too fast. And we can't run before such a sea as this, in our condition; we should be pooped in less than five minutes. We shall have to take to the boats in another couple of hours, unless a change takes place. Mr. Allen, and you, Mr. Otway, see to the two boats, and get them in readiness."

Then he went below to the passengers. They were all seated in the main cabin, and looked anxiously at him as he entered.

"I am sorry to tell you, ladies," he said quietly, "that the ship is leaking so badly that I fear we shall have to abandon her. The men cannot keep on pumping much longer, now that we are three hands short. Fortunately we have two good boats, and, if we must take to them, shall have no trouble in reaching land."

They heard him in silence, then the old priest opened his state-room door, and came out.

"That is bad news indeed, captain," he said gently. "Still we must bow to God's will, and trust to His guidance and protection. And you and your officers and crew are good and brave seamen."

"Thank you, father. We'll do all right if we have to take to the boats. And you must try and cheer up the ladies. Now I must leave you all for awhile. We will stick to the pumps for another hour or two."

"Captain," said Sarah de Boos, a tall, finely built young woman of twenty, "let my sister and myself and our servant help the men at the pump. *Do*, please. We are all three very strong, and our help is surely worth having."

Robertson patted her soft cheek with his big, sunburnt hand. "You are your father's daughter, Sarah, and I thank you. Of course your help would be something; three fine lusty young women"--he tried to smile--"but it's too dangerous for you to be on deck. All the bulwarks are gone, and nasty lumping seas come aboard every now and then."

"I'm not afraid of a life-line hurting my waist," was the prompt answer, "and neither is Sukie--are you Sukie? Go on deck, captain, and Sukie and I and Mina" (the servant) "will just kick off our boots and follow you."

"And I too," broke in old Father Roget. "Surely I am not too old to help."

In less than five minutes the two half-caste girls, the native woman Mina, and the old priest, were working the starboard brake, three seamen being on the lee side. Every now and then, as the barque took a heavy roll to windward, the water would flood her deck up to the workers' knees; but they stuck steadily to their task for half an hour, when they gave place to Burr, the carpenter, the Rev. Wilfrid, and three native seamen.

In the cabin Mrs. Lacy sat with ashen-hued face beside Miss Weidermann, their hands clasped together, and listening to the wild clamour of the wind and sea. Presently the two De Boos girls, Lacy, Father Roget, and Mina, came below to rest awhile, the water streaming from their sodden garments. The old priest, thoroughly exhausted, threw himself down upon the transom locker cushions.

"Wilfrid," said Mrs. Lacy coming over to him and placing her shaking hand on his shoulder, "cannot I do something? Oh, Miss De Boos, I wish I were brave, like you. But I am not--I am a coward, and I hate myself for it."

The Rev. Wilfrid smiled tenderly at her as he drew her to him for a moment. "Don't worry, little woman. You can't do anything--yes, you can, though! Get me my pipe and fill it for me. My hands are wet and cramped."

Sukie De Boos, whose firm, rounded bosom and strong square shoulders made a startling contrast, as they revealed their shape under her soddened blouse, to Mrs. Lacy's fragile figure, impulsively put her hands out, and taking Mrs. Lacy's face between them, kissed her twice.

"Dear Mrs. Lacy," she said, "don't be frightened, please. Now get Mr. Lacy's pipe, and I'll rummage the steward's pantry and get some food for us all to eat. Mr. Otway told me to tell you and Miss Weidermann to eat something, as maybe we may not get anything for some hours. So I'm just going to stay here and see that every one *does* eat. I'll set you a good example."

In a few minutes she laid upon the table an assortment of tinned meats, bread, and some bottled beer, and some brandy for Father Roget and Lacy. Otway came down, followed by the steward, and nodded approval.

"That's right, Sukie. Eat as much as you can. I'll take a drink myself. Here's luck to you, Sukie. Perhaps we won't have to make up a boating party after all. But there's nothing like being ready. So will you, Mr. Lacy, lend a hand here with the steward, and pass up our provisions to the second mate? The captain will be down in a minute, and will tell you ladies what clothing to get ready. For my part I'll be jolly glad if we do have to take to the boats, where we shall be nice and comfy, instead of rolling about in this beastly way--I'll be sea-sick in another ten minutes. Old Bruce says he felt sick an hour ago. Come on, steward."

The assumed cheerfulness of his manner produced a good effect, and even old Miss Weidermann plucked up heart a little as she saw him nonchalantly light a cigar as he disappeared with the steward below into the lazzarette.

On deck Robertson and the mate were talking in low tones, as they assisted the second mate with the boats. There was now nearly three feet of water in the hold, and every one knew that the barque could not keep afloat much longer. Fortunately the violence of the wind had decreased somewhat, though there was still a mountainous sea.

Both the old mate and the captain knew that the two small quarter boats would be dangerously overladen, and their unspoken fears were shared by the rest of the officers and crew. But another hour would perhaps make a great difference; and then as the two men were speaking a savage sea smote the *Tucopia* on the starboard bow, with such violence that she trembled in every timber, and as she staggered under the shock and then rolled heavily to windward, she dipped the starboard quarter boat under the water; it filled, and as she rose again, boat and davits went away together.

Robertson groaned and looked at the mate.

"It is God's will, sir," said the old Scotsman quietly.

Robertson nodded. "Tell Allen and the others to come here," he said.

The Tynesider, followed by Captain Burr, Otway, and the carpenter, came.

"Mr. Allen," said the captain, "you are the best man in such an emergency as this. You handle a boat better than any man I know. There is now only one boat left, and you must take charge of her. You will have to take a big lot of people--the four women, the parson, the old French priest, Mr. Otway, Captain Burr, the carpenter, and the five men."

"I guess I'll stand out, and stick to the ship," said Burr in a lazy, drawling manner, "I don't like bein' crowded up with a lot of wimmen."

"Neither do I, said Otway.

"Same here, captain," said the carpenter, a little grizzled man of sixty.

Robertson shook hands with each of them in turn. "I knew you were **men**," he said simply. "Come below and let's have a drink together, and then see to the boat."

"What's all this, skipper?" said Allen, with an oath, "d'ye think I'm going to save my carcase and let you men drown? I'll see you all damned first!"

"You'll obey orders," growled the captain, "and my orders are that you take charge of that boat. And don't give me any lip. You are a married man and have children. None of us who are standing by the ship are married men. By God, my joker, if you don't know your duty, I'll teach you. Are you going to let these four women go adrift in a boat to perish when you can save them?"

Allen looked the captain squarely in the face and then put out his hand.

"I understand you, sir. But I don't like doing it. The ship won't keep afloat another hour. But, as you say, I've a wife and kids to consider."

*   *   *   *   *

Followed by the others, Robertson went below, and told his passengers to get ready for the boat. The old French priest, exhausted by his labour at the pumps, was still lying on the transom cushions, sleeping; the Rev. Lacy was seated at the table smoking his pipe (all the ladies were in their state-rooms). He rose as the men entered, and looked at them inquiringly.

"We're in a bit of a tight place," said the captain, as he coolly poured out half a tumblerful of brandy, "but I'm sending you, Mr. Lacy, and Father Roget, and the ladies away with Mr. Allen in one of the boats. Allen is a man whom I rely upon. He'll bring you ashore safely. He's a bit rough in his talk, but he's one of God's own chosen in a boat, and a fine sailor man--better than the mate, Captain Burr, or myself; isn't that so, Mr. Bruce?"

The white-haired old mate bent his head in acknowledgment. Then he stood up stiff and stark, his rough bony hands clasped upon his chest.

"I'll no' deny but that Mr. Allen is far and awa' the best man to have charge o' the boat. But as there is a meenister here, surely he will now offer up a prayer to the Almighty for those in peril on the sea, and especially implore Him to consider a sma' boat, deep to the gunwales."

He looked at the clergyman, who at first made no reply, but stood with downcast eyes. The men looked at him expectantly; he put one hand on the table, and then slowly raised his face.

"I think, gentlemen, that ... that Father Roget is the older man." He spoke haltingly, and a flush dyed his smooth, clean-shaven face from brow to chin. "Will you not ask him?" Then his eyes dropped again.

Robertson, who was in a hurry, and yet had a sincere but secret respect for old Bruce's unobtrusive religious feelings, now backed up his mate's request.

"I think, sir, that as the mate says, a bit of a short prayer would not be out of place just now, seeing the mess we are in. And that poor old gentleman over there is too done up to stand on his feet. So will you please begin, sir. Steward, call the ladies. We can no longer disguise from them, Mr. Lacy, that we are in a bad way--as bad a way as I have ever been in during my thirty years at sea."

In a couple of minutes the two De Boos girls, Miss Weidermann, and the native girl Mina, came out of their cabins; and when the steward said that Mrs. Lacy felt too ill to leave her berth, her husband could not help giving an audible sigh of relief. Then he braced up and spoke with firmness.

"Please shut Mrs. Lacy's door, steward. Mr. Bruce, will you lend me your church service--I do not want to go into my cabin for my own. My wife, I fear, has given way."

The mate brought the church service, and then whilst the men stood with bowed heads, and the women knelt, the clergyman, with strong, unfaltering voice read the second of the prayers "To be used in Storms at Sea." He finished, and then sitting down again, placed one hand over his eyes.

"*The living, the living shall praise Thee*."

It was the old mate who spoke. He alone of the men had knelt beside the women, and when he rose his face bore such an expression of calmness and content, that Otway, who five minutes before had been silently cursing him for his "damned idiotcy," looked at him with a sudden mingled respect and wonder.

Stepping across to the clergyman, Bruce respectfully placed his hand on his shoulder, and as he spoke his clear blue eyes smiled at the still kneeling women.

"Cheer up, sir. God will protect ye and your gude wife, and us all. You, his meenister, have made supplication to Him, and He has heard. Dinna weep, ladies. We are in the care of One who holds the sea in the hollow of His hand."

Then he followed the captain and the others on deck, Otway alone remaining to assist the steward.

"For God's sake give me some brandy," said Lacy to him, in a low voice.

Otway looked at him in astonishment. Was the man a coward after all?

He brought the brandy, and with ill-disguised contempt placed it before him without a word. Lacy looked up at him, and his face flushed.

"Oh, I'm not funking--not a d----d bit, I can assure you."

Otway at once poured out a nip of brandy for himself, and clinked his glass against that of the clergyman.

"Pon my soul, I couldn't make it out, and I apologise. But a man's nerves go all at once sometimes--can't help himself, you know. Mine did once when I was in the nigger-catching business in the Solomon Islands. Natives opened fire on us when our boats were aground in a creek, and some of our men got hit. I wasn't a bit scared of a smack from a bullet, but when I got a scratch on my hand from an arrow, I dropped in a blue funk, and acted like a cur. Knew it was poisoned, felt sure I'd die of lockjaw, and began to weep internally. Then the mate called me a rotten young cur, shook me up, and put my Snider into my hand. But I shall always feel funky at the sight even of a child's twopenny bow and arrow. Now I must go."

The clergyman nodded and smiled, and then rising from his seat, he tapped at the door of his wife's state-room. She opened it, and then Otway, who was helping the steward, heard her sob hysterically.

"Oh, Will, Will, why did you? How could you? I love you, Will dear, I love you, and if death comes to us in another hour, another minute, I shall die happily with your arms round me. But, Will dear, there is a God, I'm sure there *is* a God.... I feel it in my heart, I feel it. And now that death is so near to us----"

Lacy put his arms around her, and lifted her trembling figure upon his knees.

"There, rest yourself, my pet."

"Rest! Rest?" she said brokenly, as Lacy drew her to him. "How can I rest when I think of how I have sinned, and how I shall die! Will dear, when I heard you reading that prayer--"

"I *had* to do it, Nell."

"Will, dear Will.... Perhaps God may forgive us both.... But as I sat here in my dark cabin, and listened to you reading that prayer, my husband's face came before me--the face that I thought was so dull and stupid. And his eyes seemed so soft and kind--"

"For God's sake, my dear little woman, don't think of what is past. We have made the plunge together----"

The woman uttered one last sobbing sigh. "I am not afraid to die, Will. I am not afraid, but when I heard you begin to read that prayer, my courage forsook me. I wanted to scream--to rush out and stop you, for it seemed to me as if you were doing it in sheer mockery."

"I can only say again, Nell, that I could not help myself; made me feel pretty sick, I assure you."

Their voices ceased, and presently Lacy stepped out into the main cabin, and then went on deck again.

Robertson met him with a cheerful face. "Come on, Mr. Lacy. I've some good news for you--we are making less water! The leak must be taking up in some way." Then holding on to the rail with one hand, he shouted to the men at the pumps.

"Shake her up, boys! shake her up. Here's Mr. Lacy come to lend a hand, and the supercargo and steward will be with you in a minute. Now I'm going below for a minute to tell the ladies, and mix you a bucket of grog. Shake her up, you, Tom Tarbucket, my bully boy with a glass eye! Shake her up, and when she sucks dry, I'll stand a sovereign all round."

The willing crew answered him with a cheer, and Tom Tarbucket, a square-built, merry faced native of Savage Island, who was stripped to the waist, shouted out, amid the laughter of his shipmates--

"Ay, ay, capt'in, we soon make pump suck dry if two Miss de Boos girl come."

Robertson laughed in response, and then picking up a wooden bucket from under the fife rail, clattered down the companion way.

"Where are you, Otway? Up you get on deck, and you too, steward. The leak is taken up and 'everything is lovely and the goose hangs high.' Up you go to the pumps, and make 'em suck. I'll bring up some grog presently."

Then as Otway and the steward sprang up on deck, the captain stamped along the cabin in his sodden sea boots, banging at each door.

"Come out, Sarah, come out Sukie, my little chickabiddies--there's to be no boat trip for you after all. Miss Weidermann, I've good news, good news! Mrs. Lacy, cheer up, dear lady. The leak has taken up, and you can go on deck and see your husband working at the pumps like a number one chop Trojan. Ha! Father Roget, give me your hand. You're a white man, sir, and ought to be a bishop."

As he spoke to the now awakened old priest, the two De Boos girls, Mrs. Lacy and Miss Weidermann, all came out of their cabins, and Robertson shook hands with them, and lifting Sukie de Boos up between his two rough hands as if she were a little girl, he kissed her, and then made a grab at Sarah, who dodged behind Mrs. Lacy.

"Now, father, don't you attempt to come on deck. Mrs. Lacy, just you keep him here. Sukie, my chick, you and Sarah get a couple of bottles of brandy, make this bucket full of half-and-half, and bring it on deck to the men."

As he noisily stamped out of the cabin again, the old priest turned to the ladies, and raised his hand--

"A brave, brave man--a very good English sailor. And now let us thank God for His mercies to us."

The four ladies, with Mina, knelt, and then the good old man prayed fervently for a few minutes. Then Sukie de Boos and her sister flung their arms around Mrs. Lacy, and kissed her, and even Miss Weidermann, now thoroughly unstrung, began to cry hysterically. She had at first detested Mrs. Lacy as being altogether too scandalously young and pretty for a clergyman's wife. Now she was ready to take her to her bosom (that is, to her metaphorical bosom, as she had no other), for she believed that Mr. Lacy's prayer had saved them all, he being a Protestant clergyman, and therefore better qualified to avert imminent death than a priest of Rome.

Sukie and Sally de Boos mixed the grog, took it on deck, and served it out to the men at the pumps.

The carpenter sounded the well, and as he drew up the iron rod, the second mate gave a shout.

"Only seven inches, captain."

"Right, my boy. Take a good spell now, Mr. Allen. Mr. Bruce, we can give her a bit more lower canvas now. She'll stand it. Mr. Lacy, and you Captain Burr, come aft and get into some dry togs. The glass is rising steadily, and in a few hours we'll feel a bit more comfy."

He prophesied truly, for the violence of the gale decreased rapidly, and when at the end of an hour the pumps sucked, the crew gave a cheer, and tired out as they were, eagerly sprang aloft to repair damages and then spread more sail, Sarah and

Susan de Boos hauling and pulling at the running gear from the deck below. They were both girls of splendid physique, and, in a way, sailors, and had Robertson allowed them to do so, would have gone aloft and handled the canvas with the men.

By four o'clock in the afternoon the little barque, with her wave-swept, bulwarkless decks, now drying under a bright sun, was running before a warm, good-hearted breeze, and the pumps were only attended to twice in every watch.

Mrs. Lacy, Miss Weidermann, the De Boos girls, and the French priest were seated on the poop deck, on rugs and blankets spread out for them by Otway and the steward. Lacy, with Captain Burr, was pacing to and fro smoking his pipe, and laughing heartily at Sukie de Boos's attempts to make his wife smoke a cigarette. Presently old Bruce came along with the second mate and some men to set a new gaff-topsail, and the ladies rose to go below, so as to be out of the way.

"Nae, nae, leddies, dinna go below," said the old mate cheerfully, "ye'll no' hinder us. And the sight o' sae many sweet, bonny faces will mak' us work a' the better. And how are ye now, Mrs. Lacy? Ah, the pink roses are in your cheeks once mair." And then he stepped quickly up to the young clergyman and took his hand.

"Mr. Lacy, ye must pardon me, but I'm an auld man, and must hae my way. Ye're a gude, brave man;" then he added in a low voice, "and ye called upon Him, and He heard us."

"Thank you, Mr. Bruce," Lacy answered nervously, as he saw his wife's eyes droop, and a vivid blush dye her fair cheeks. Then he plucked the American captain by the sleeve and went below, and Sukie de Boos laughed loudly when in another minute they heard the pop of a bottle of soda water. She ran to the skylight and bent down.

"You're a pair of exceedingly rude men. You might think of Father Roget--even if you don't think of us poor women. Mr. Otway, come here, you horrid, dirty-faced, ragged creature! Go below and get a glass of port wine for Father Roget, a bottle of champagne for Mrs. Lacy and my sister and myself, and a cup of tea for Mrs. Weidermann, and bring some biscuits, too."

"Come and help me, then," said the supercargo, who was indeed dirty-faced and ragged.

Sukie danced towards the companion way with him. Half-way down he put his arms round her and kissed her vigorously. She returned his kisses with interest, and laughingly smacked his cheek.

"Let me go, Charlie Otway, you horrid, bold fellow. Now, one, two, three, or I'll call out and invoke the protection of the clergy, above and below--those on board this ship I mean, not those who are in heaven or elsewhere."

*   *   *   *   *

Ten days later the *Tucopia* sailed into Apia Harbour and dropped anchor inside Matautu Point just as the evening mists were closing their fleecy mantle around the verdant slopes of Vailima Mountain.

The two half-caste girls, with their maid and Mr. and Mrs. Lacy, came to bid Otway and the captain a brief farewell, before they went ashore in the pilot boat to D'Acosta's hotel in Matafele.

"Now remember, Otway, and you, Captain Robertson, and you, Captain Burr, you are all to dine with us at the hotel the day after to-morrow. And perhaps you, too, Father Roget will reconsider your decision and come too." It was Lacy who spoke.

The gentle-voiced old Frenchman shook his head and smiled--"Ah no, it was impossible," he said. The bishop would not like him to so soon leave the Mission. But the bishop and his brothers at the Mission would look forward to have the good captain, and Mr. Burr, and Mr. Otway, and the ladies to accept his hospitality.

Mrs. Lacy's soft little gloved hand was in Otway's.

"I thank you, Mr. Otway, very, very sincerely for your many kindnesses to me. You have indeed been most generous to us both. It was cruel of us to take your cabin and compel you to sleep in the trade-room. But I shall never forget how kind you have been."

All that was good in Otway came into his vicious heart and voiced softly through his lips.

"I am only too glad, Mrs. Lacy.... I am indeed. I didn't like giving up my cabin to strangers at first, and was a bit of a beast when Mr. Harry told me we were taking two extra passengers. But I am glad now."

He turned away, and went below with burning cheeks. Before the storm he had tried his best, late on several nights, to make Lacy drunk, and to keep him drunk; but Lacy could stand as much or more grog than he could himself; and when he heard that passionate, sobbing appeal, "Oh, Will, Will, how could you?" his better nature was stirred, and his fierce sensual desire for her changed into a sentimental affection and respect. He knew her secret, and now, instead of wishing to take advantage of it, felt he was too much of a man to abuse his knowledge.

*   *   *   *   *

Supper was over, and as the skipper, Burr, and Otway paced the quarter-deck before going ashore to play a game or two of billiards and meet some friends, a boat came alongside, and a man stepped on deck and inquired for the captain. As he followed Robertson down the companion, Otway saw that he was a well-dressed, rather gentlemanly-looking young man of about five and twenty.

"Who's that joker, I wonder?" he said to Burr; "not any one living in Samoa, unless he's a new-comer. Hope he won't stay long--it's eight o'clock now."

Ten minutes later the steward came to him.

"The captain wishes to see you, sir."

Otway entered the cabin. Robertson, with frowning face, motioned him to a seat. The strange gentleman sat near the captain smoking a cigar, and with some papers in his hands.

"Mr. Otway, I have sent for you. This gentleman has a warrant for the arrest of Mr. Lacy, issued by the New Zealand Government and initialled by the British Consul here."

Otway rose to the occasion. He nodded to the stranger and sat down quietly.

"Yes, sir?" he asked inquiringly of Robertson.

"You will please tell my supercargo your business, mister," said the captain gruffly to the stranger; "he can tell you all you wish to know--that is, if he cares to do so. I don't see that your warrant holds any force here in Samoa. You can't execute it. There's no government here, no police, no anything, and the British Consul can't act on a warrant issued from New Zealand. It is of no more use in Samoa than it would be at Cape Horn."

"Now, sir, make haste," said Otway with a mingled and studied insolence and politeness. He already began to detest the stranger.

"I am a detective of the police force of New Zealand, and I have come from Auckland to arrest William Barton, alias the Rev. Wilfrid Lacy, on a charge of stealing twenty thousand, five hundred pounds from the National Bank of Christchurch, of which he was manager. I believe that twenty thousand pounds of the money he has stolen is on board this vessel at this moment, and I now demand access to his cabin."

"Do you? How are you going to enforce your demand, my cocksure friend?"

Otway rose, and placing his two hands on the table, looked insultingly at the detective. "What rot you are talking, man!"

The detective drew back, alarmed and startled.

"The British Consul has endorsed my warrant to arrest this man," he said, "and it will go hard with any one who attempts to interfere with me in the performance of my duty."

Otway shot a quick, triumphant glance at the captain.

"The Consul is, and always was, a silly old ass. You have come on a fool's errand; and are going on the wrong tack by making threats. That idiotic warrant of yours is of no more use to you than a sheet of fly paper--Samoa is outside British jurisdiction. The High Commissioner for the Western Pacific would not have endorsed such a fool of a document, and I'll report the matter to him.... Now, sit down and tell me what you *do* want, and I'll try and help you all I can. But don't try to bluff us--it's only wasting your time. Steward, bring us something to drink."

As soon as the steward brought them "something to drink" Otway became deeply sympathetic with the detective, and Robertson, who knew his supercargo well, smiled inwardly at the manner he adopted.

"Now, just tell us, Mr.--O'Donovan, I think you said is your name--what is all the trouble? I need hardly tell you that whilst both the captain and myself felt annoyed at your dictatorial manner, we are both sensible men, and will do all in our power to assist you. Our firm's reputation has to be studied--has it not, captain? We don't want it to be insinuated that we helped an embezzler to escape, do we?"

"Certainly not," replied Robertson, puffing slowly at his cigar, watching Otway keenly through his half-closed eyelids, and wondering what that astute young gentleman was driving at. "I guess that you, Mr. Otway, will do all that is right and cor-rect."

"Thank you, sir," replied Otway humbly, and with great seriousness, "I know my duty to my employers, and I know that this gentleman may be led into very serious trouble through the dense stupidity of the British Consul here."

He turned to Mr. O'Donovan--"Are you aware, Mr. O'Donikin--I beg your pardon, O'Donovan--that the British Consul here is not, officially, the British Consul. He is merely a commercial agent, like the United States Consul. Neither are accredited by their Governments to act officially on behalf of their respective countries, and even if they were, there is no extradition treaty with the Samoan Islands, which is a country without a recognised government. Of course, Mr. O'Donovan, you are acting in good faith; but you have no more legal right nor the power to arrest a man in Samoa, than you have to arrest one in Manchuria or Patagonia. Of course, old Johns (the British Consul) doesn't know this, or he would not have made such a fool of himself by endorsing a warrant from an irresponsible judge of a New Zealand court. But as I told you, I shall aid you in every possible way."

O'Donovan was no fool. He knew that all that Otway had said was absolutely correct, but he braced himself up.

"I daresay what you say may be right, Mr. Supercargo. But I've come from New Zealand to get this joker, and by blazes I mean to get him, and take him back with me to New Zealand. And I mean to have those twenty thousand sovereigns to take back as well."

"Well, then, why the devil don't you go and get your man? He's at Joe D'Acosta's hotel with his wife."

"I don't want to be bothered with him just yet. I have no place to put him into. The Californian mail boat from San Francisco is not due here for another ten days. But I know that he hasn't taken his stolen money ashore yet, and you had better hand it over to me at once. I can get *him* at any time."

Otway leant back in his chair and laughed.

"I don't doubt that, Mr. O'Donovan. If you have enough money to do it, you can do as you say--get this man at any time. But you want to have some guns behind you to enforce it; and then his capture won't affect our custody of the money. If the Consul instigates you to make an attack on the ship, you will do so at your peril, for we shall resist any piratical attempt."

O'Donovan's face fell. "You said you would assist me?"

"So I will," replied Otway, lying genially, "But you must point out a way. The High Commissioner for the Western Pacific, in Fiji, is the only man who could give you power to arrest the man and convey him to New Zealand, and the moment you show me the High or the Deputy High Commissioner's order to hand over the money, and Lacy's other effects, I'll do so."

The detective made his last stroke.

"I can take the law into my own hands and chance the consequences. The Consul will supply me with a force--"

Robertson smiled grimly, and pointed to the rack of Snider rifles around the mizen-mast at the head of the table.

"You and your force will have a bad time of it then, and be shot down before you can put foot on my deck. I've never seen a shark eat a policeman, but there seems a chance of it now."

O'Donovan laughed uneasily, then he changed his tactics.

"Now look here, gentlemen," he said confidentially, leaning across the table, "I can see I'm in a bit of a hole, but I'm a business man, and you are business men, and I think we understand one another, eh? As you say, my warrant doesn't hold good here in Samoa. But the Consul will back me up, and if I can take this chap back to New Zealand it means a big thing for me. Now, what's your figure?"

"Two hundred each for the skipper and myself," answered Otway promptly.

"Done. You shall have it."

"When?"

"Give me till to-morrow afternoon. I've only a hundred and fifty pounds with me, and I'll have to raise the rest."

"Very well, it's a deal. But mind, you'll have to take care to be here before the parson. He's coming off at eleven o'clock."

"Trust me for that, gentlemen."

"I'm sorry for his wife," said Otway meditatively.

O'Donovan grinned. "Ah, I haven't told you the yarn--she's not his wife! She bolted from her husband, who is a big swell in Auckland, a Mr.----."

"How did you get on their tracks?"

"Sydney police found out that two people answering their description had sailed for the Islands in the *Tucopia*, and cabled over to us. We thought they had lit out for America. I only got here the day before yesterday in the **Ryno**, from Auckland."

Otway paid him some very florid compliments on his smartness, and then after another drink or two, the detective went on shore, highly pleased.

As soon as he was gone, Otway turned to Robertson.

"You won't stand in my way, Robertson, will you?" he asked--"I want to see the poor devils get away."

"You take all the responsibility, then."

"I will," and then he rapidly told the skipper his plan, and set to work by at once asking the second mate to get ready the boat and then come back to the cabin.

"All ready," said Allen, five minutes later.

"Then come with the steward and help me with this gear."

He unlocked the door of Lacy's state-room, lit the swinging candle, and quickly passed out Mr. and Mrs. Lacy's remaining luggage to the second mate and steward. Three small leather trunks, marked "Books with Care," were especially heavy, and he guessed their contents.

"Stow them safely in the boat, Allen. Don't make more noise than you can help. I'll be with you in a minute."

Going into his own cabin, he took a large handbag, threw into it his revolver and two boxes of cartridges, then carried it into the trade-room, and added half a dozen tins of the brand of tobacco which he knew Lacy liked, and then filled the remaining space with pint bottles of champagne. Then he whipped up a sheet or two of letter paper and an envelope from the cabin-table, thrust them into his coat pocket, and, bag in hand, stepped quickly on deck. The old mate was in his cabin, and had not heard anything.

"Give it to her, boys," he said to the crew, taking the steer-oar in his hand, and heading the boat towards a small fore-and-aft schooner lying half a mile away in the Matafele horn of the reef encircling Apia Harbour.

The four native seamen bent to their oars in silence, and sped swiftly through the darkness over the calm waters of the harbour. The schooner showed no riding light on her forestay, but, on the after deck under the awning, a lamp was burning, and three men--the captain, mate, and boatswain--were playing cards on the skylight.

Otway jumped on deck, just as the men rose to meet him.

"Great Ascensial Jehosophat! Why, it's you, Mr. Otway?" cried the captain, a little clean-shaven man, as he shook hands with the supercargo. "Well, now, I was just wondering whether I'd go ashore and try and drop across you. Say, tell me now, hev you any good tinned beef and a case of Winchesters you can sell me?"

"Yes, both," replied Otway, shaking hands with the three in turn--they were all old acquaintances, especially Le Brun, the mate. "But come below with me, Revels; I've important business, and it has to be done right away--this very night."

Revels led the way below into the schooner's cabin, and at once produced a bottle of Bourbon and a couple of glasses.

"No time to drink, Revels.... All right, just a little, then. Now, tell me, do you want to make--and make it easy--five hundred pounds?"

"Guess I do."

"Are you ready for sea?"

"I was thinking of sailing on a cruise among the Tokelau Islands in a day or two."

"Then don't think of it. If you put to sea to-night for a longer voyage, I can guarantee you that you will get five hundred pounds--if you will take two passengers on board, and put to sea as soon as they come alongside."

"Where do they want to go?"

"That I can't say. Manila or Hongkong, most likely. It'll pay you."

"Is the money safe?"

Otway struck his hand on the table. "Safe as rain, Revels. They have plenty. I have it here alongside, and if you don't get five hundred sovereigns paid you when you have dropped Samoa astern, you can come back with your passengers, and I'll give you fifty pounds myself."

"Friends of yours?"

"Yes."

"That's enough fur me, Otway. Now, just tell me what to do."

"Tell your mate to get your boat ready to go ashore, while I write a note."

He took a sheet of paper, and hurriedly wrote in pencil:

"DEAR LACY,--Don't hesitate to follow my instructions. There's a man here from New Zealand. Tried to get access to your cabin; bluffed him. You and your wife must follow bearer of this note to his boat, which will bring you to a schooner. The captain's name is Revels. He expects you, and you can trust him. Have pledged him my word that you will give him L500 to land you at Manila or thereabouts; also that you will hand it to him as soon as the schooner is clear of the land. *All* your luggage is on board the schooner, awaiting you. Allen helped me. You might send him a present by Revels. Goodbye, and all good luck. One last word--***be quick, be quick***!"

"Boat is ready," said Revels.

"Right," and Otway closed the letter and handed it to the mate. "Here you are, Le Brun. Now, listen. Pull in to the mouth of the creek at the French Mission, just beside the bridge. Leave your boat there and then take this letter to D'Acosta's Hotel and ask to see Mr. Lacy. If he and his wife have gone out for a walk, you must follow them and give him the letter; but I feel pretty sure you'll find them on the verandah. Bring them off on board as quickly and as quietly as possible. No one will take any notice of the boat in the creek. Oh! and tell Mr. Lacy to be dead sure not to bring anything in the way of even a small bag with him--Joe D'Acosta might wonder. I'll settle the hotel bill later on. Are you clear?"

"Clear as mud," replied Le Brun, a big, black-whiskered Guernsey man.

"Then goodbye."

The schooner's boat, manned by two hands only, pushed off, and then Revels turned to Otway.

"Shall I heave short so as to be ready?"

"Heave short, be d----d!" replied Otway testily. "No, just lie nice and quiet, and as soon as you have your passengers on board slip your cable. I'll see that your anchor is fished up for you. And even if you lost your anchor and a few fathoms of chain it doesn't matter against five hundred sovereigns. The people on shore would be sure to hear the sound of the windlass pawls, and there's a man here from Auckland--a detective--who might make a bold stroke, get a dozen native bullies and collar you. So slip, my boy, slip. There's a fine healthy breeze which will take you clear of the reef in ten minutes."

The two men shook hands, and Otway stepped into his boat, which he steered in towards the principal jetty.

Jumping out he walked along the roadway which led from Matafele to Apia. As he passed the British Consul's house he saw Mr. O'Donovan standing on the verandah talking to the Consul. He waved his hand to them, and cheerfully invited the detective to come along to "Johnnie Hall's" and play a game of billiards.

Mr. O'Donovan, little thinking that Otway had a purpose in view, took the bait. The Consul knew Otway, and, in a measure, dreaded him, for the supercargo's knowledge of certain transactions in connection with the sale of arms to natives, in which he (the Consul) had taken a leading and lucrative part. So when he saw the supercargo of the *Tucopia* beckoning to O'Donovan he smiled genially at him, and hurriedly told the detective to go.

"He's a most astute and clever young scoundrel, Mr. O'Donovan, and in a way we are at his mercy. But you shall have the four hundred pounds in the morning-- not later than noon. This man Barton must be brought to justice at any cost."

"Just so, sir; and you will get a hundred out of the business, any way," replied O'Donovan, who had gauged the Consul's morality pretty fairly.

As Otway and the detective walked towards the hotel known as "Johnny Hall's" the former said lazily--

"Look here, Mr. O'Donovan. Are the skipper and myself to get those four hundred sovs to-morrow or not? To tell you the exact truth, I have a fair amount of doubt about your promise. Where are you going to get the money?"

"That's all right, Mr. Otway. You're a business man. And you and the skipper will have your two hundred each before one o'clock to-morrow. The Consul is doing the necessary."

"Right, my boy," said Otway effusively. "Now we'll play a game or two at Johnny's and have some fun with the girls."

By eleven o'clock Mr. O'Donovan was comfortably half drunk, and Otway led him out on to the verandah to look at the harbour, shimmering under the starlight. They sat down on two cane lounges, and the supercargo's keen eye saw that Revel's schooner had gone. He breathed freely, and then brought Mr. O'Donovan a large whisky and soda.

*   *   *   *   *

In the morning Mr. O'Donovan and Mr. William Johns, the British Consul, were in a state of frenzy on discovering that Mr. and Mrs. Lacy had escaped during the night in the schooner *Solafanua*. The Consul knew that Otway was at the bottom of the matter, but dared not say so, but O'Donovan, who had more pluck and nothing to lose, lost his temper and came on board the *Tucopia* just as she was being hauled up on the beach to get at the leak.

"You're a dirty sweep," he said to Otway.

The supercargo hit him between the eyes, and sent him down. Allen picked him up, dumped him into the boat alongside, and sent him ashore.

When the *Tucopia* lay high and dry on Apia beach Otway and old Bruce walked round under her counter and looked for the leak. As the skipper had surmised, a butt-end had started, but the gaping orifice was now choked and filled with a large piece of seaweed.

"The prayer of one of God's ain ministers has saved us," said the Scotch mate, pointing upward.

"No doubt," replied Otway, who knew that the good old man had heard nothing of what had happened.

The Man in the Buffalo Hide

Twelve years ago in a North Queensland town I was told the story of "The Man in the Buffalo Hide" by Ned D----. He (D----) was then a prosperous citizen, having made a small fortune by "striking it rich" on the Gilbert and Etheridge Rivers goldfields. Returning from the arid wastes of the Queensland back country to Sydney, he tired of leading an inactive life, and hearing that gold had been discovered on one of the Solomon Islands, he took passage thither in the Sydney whaling barque ***Costa Rica*** packet, and though he returned to Australia without discovering gold in the islands, he had kept one of the most interesting logs of a whaling cruise it has ever been my fortune to read. The master of the whaleship was Captain J.Y. Carpenter, a man who is well known and highly respected, not only in Sydney (where he now resides), but throughout the East Indies and China, where he had lived for over thirty years. And it was from Captain Carpenter who was one of the actors in this twice-told tragedy, that D----heard this story of Chinese vengeance. He (D----) related it to me in '88, and I wish I could write the tale as well and vividly as he told it. However, I wrote it out for him then and there. Much to our disgust the editor of the little journal to whom we sent the MS., considered it a fairy tale, and cut it down to some two or three hundred words. I mention these apparently unnecessary details merely that the reader may not think that the tale is fiction, for two years or so after, Captain Carpenter corroborated my friend's story.

*   *   *   *   *

It was after the Taeping rebellion had been stamped out in blood and fire by Gordon and his "Ever Victorious Army," and the Viceroy (Li Hung Chang) had taken up his quarters in Canton, and was secretly torturing and beheading those prisoners whom he had sworn to the English Government to spare.

Carpenter was in command of a Chinese Government despatch vessel--a side-wheeler--which was immediately under the Viceroy's orders. She was but lightly armed, but was very fast, as fast went in those days. His ship had been lying in the filthy river for about a week, when, one afternoon, a mandarin came off with a written order for him to get ready to proceed to sea at daylight on the following morning. Previous experience of his estimable and astute Chinese employers warned him not to ask the fat-faced, almond-eyed mandarin any questions as to the steamer's destination, or the duration of the voyage. He simply said that he would be ready at the appointed time.

At daylight another mandarin, named Kwang--one of much higher rank than his visitor of the previous day--came on board. He was attended by thirty of the most ruffianly-looking scoundrels--even for Chinamen--that the captain had ever seen. They were all well armed, and came off in a large, well-appointed boat, which, the mandarin intimated with a polite smile, was to be towed, if she was too heavy to be hoisted aboard. A couple of hands were put in her, and she was veered astern. Then the anchor was lifted, and the steamer started on her eighty miles trip down the river to the sea, the mandarin informing the captain that he would name the ship's destination as soon as they were clear of the land.

Most of Carpenter's officers were Europeans--Englishmen or Americans--and one or two of them who spoke Chinese, attempted to enter into conversation with the thirty braves, and endeavour to learn the object of the steamer's mission. Their inquiries were met either with a mocking jest or downright insult, and presently the mandarin, who hitherto had preserved a smiling and affable demeanour as he sat on the quarter-deck, turned to the captain with a sullen and ferocious aspect, and bade him remind his officers that they had no business to question the servants of the "high and excellent Viceroy."

But though neither Carpenter nor any of his officers could learn aught about this sudden mission, one of their servants, a Chinese who was deeply attached to his master, whispered tremblingly to him that the mandarin and the thirty braves were in quest of one of the Viceroy's most hated enemies--a noted leader of the Taepings who had escaped the bloodied hands of Li Hung Chang, and whose retreat had been betrayed to the cruel, merciless Li the previous day.

Once clear of the land, the mandarin, with a polite smile and many compliments to Carpenter on the skilful and expeditious manner in which he had navigated the steamer down the river, requested him to proceed to a certain point on the western side of the island of Formosa.

"When you are within twenty miles of the land, captain," he said suavely, "you will make the steamer stop, and my men and I will leave you in the boat. You must await our return, which may be on the following day, or the day after, or perhaps longer still. But whether I am absent one, or two, or six days, you must keep your ship in the position I indicate as nearly as possible. You must avoid observation from the shore, you must be watchful, diligent, and patient, and, when you see my boat returning, you must make your engines work quickly, and come towards us with all speed. High commendation and a great reward from the serene nobleness of our great Viceroy--who has already condescended to notice your honourable ability and great integrity in your profession--awaits you." Then with another smile and bow he went to his cabin.

As soon as the steamer reached the place indicated by the mandarin the engines were stopped. The boat, which was towing astern, was hauled alongside, and the thirty truculent "braves," with a Chinese pilot and the ever-smiling mandarin, got into her and pushed off for the shore. That they were all picked men, who could handle an oar as well as a rifle, was very evident from the manner in which they sent the big boat along towards the blue outline of the distant shore.

*   *   *   *   *

For two days Carpenter and his officers waited and watched, the steamer lying and rolling about upon a long swell, and under a hot and brazen sun. Then, about seven o'clock in the morning, as the sea haze lifted, a look-out on the foreyard hailed the deck and said the boat was in sight. The steamer's head was at once put towards her under a full head of steam, and in another hour the mandarin and his braves were alongside.

The mandarin clambered up on deck, his always-smiling face (which Carpenter and his officers had come to detest) now darkly exultant.

"You have done well, sir," he said to the captain; "the Viceroy himself, when my own miserable worthlessness abases itself before him, shall know how truly and cleverly you and your officers (who shall be honoured for countless ages in the future) have obeyed the behests which I have had the never-to-be-extinguished honour to convey from him to you. There is a prisoner in the boat--a prisoner who is to be tried before those high and merciful judges whose Heaven-sent authority your valorous commander of the Ever Victorious Army has upheld."

Carpenter, being a sailor man before all else, swallowed the mandarin's compliments for all they were worth, and I can imagine him giving a grumpy nod to the smiling minion of the Viceroy as he ordered "the prisoner" to be brought on deck, and the boat to be veered astern for towing.

The official interposed oilily. There was no need, he said, to tow the boat to Canton if she could not be hoisted on board, and was likely to impede the steamer's progress. Some of his braves could remain in her, and the insignia of the Viceroy which they wore would ensure both their and the boat's safety--no pirates would touch them.

The captain said that to tow such a heavy boat for such a long distance would certainly delay the steamer's arrival in Canton by at least six or eight hours. The mandarin smiled sweetly, and said that as speed was everything the most honourable navigator, whom he now had the privilege to address, and who was so soon to be distinguished by his mightiness the Viceroy, could at once let the boat which had conveyed his worthless self into the sunshine of his (the captain's) presence, go adrift.

At a sign from Kwang, six of his cutthroats clambered down the side into the boat, which was at once cast off; the steamer was sent along under a full head of steam, and the captain was about to ascend the bridge when the mandarin stayed him, and requested that a meal should be at once prepared in the cabin for the prisoner, who, he said, was somewhat exhausted, for his capture was only effected after he had killed three and wounded half a dozen of "the braves." So courageous a man, he added softly, whatever his offence might be, must not be allowed to suffer the pangs of hunger and thirst.

Carpenter gave the necessary order to the steward with a sensation of pleasure, feeling that he had done the suave and gentle-voiced Kwang an injustice in imagining him to be like most Chinese officials--utterly indifferent and callous to human suffering. Then he stepped along the deck towards the bridge just as two of the braves lifted the prisoner to his feet, which a third had freed from a thong of hide, bound so tightly around them that it had literally cut into the flesh. His hands were tied in the same manner, and round his neck was an iron collar, with a chain about six feet in length which was secured at the end to another band around the waist of one of the "braves."

As the prisoner stood erect, Carpenter saw that he was a man of herculean proportions and over six feet three or four inches in height. His arms and naked chest were cut, bleeding and bruised, and a bamboo gag was in his mouth; but what at once attracted the captain's attention and sympathy was the man's face.

So calm, steadfast, and serene were his clear, undaunted eyes; so proud, lofty, and contemptuous and yet so dignified his bearing, as he glanced at his guards when they bade him walk, that Carpenter, drawing back a little, raised his hand in salute.

In an instant the deep, dark eyes lit up, and the tortured, distorted mouth would have smiled had it not been for the cruel gag. But twice he bent his head, and his eyes did that which was denied to his lips.

Captain Carpenter was deeply moved. The man's heroic fortitude, his noble bearing under such physical suffering, the tender, woman-like resignation in the eyes which could yet smile into his, affected him so strongly that he could not help asking one of the "braves" the prisoner's name.

An insolent, threatening gesture was the only answer. But the prisoner had heard, and bent his head in acknowledgment. When he raised it again and saw that Carpenter had now taken off his cap, tears trickled down his cheeks. In another moment he was hurried along the deck into the cabin, and half a dozen "braves" stood guard at the door to prevent intrusion, whilst the gag was removed, and the victim of the Viceroy's vengeance was urged to eat. Whether he did so or not was never known, for half an hour afterwards he was removed to one of the state-rooms, where he was closely guarded by Kwang's cutthroats. When he was next seen by Carpenter and the officers of the steamer the gag was again in his mouth, but the calm, resolute eyes met theirs as it trying to tell them that the heroic soul within the tortured body knew no fear, and felt and appreciated their sympathy.

On the afternoon of the third day after leaving Formosa the steamer ploughed her way up the muddy waters of the river, and came to an anchor off the city at a place which was within half a mile of the Viceroy's residence. The mandarin requested the captain to fire three guns, and hoist the Chinese flag at both the fore and main peaks.

This signal was, so Kwang condescended to say, to inform His Illustriousness the Ever-Merciful Viceroy that he, Kwang, his crawling dependent, guided by Carpenter's high intelligence, and supreme and honoured skill as a navigator, had achieved the object which His Illustriousness desired.

The captain listened to all this "flam," bowed his acknowledgments, and then suddenly asked the mandarin the prisoner's name.

Again the fat, complacent face darkened, and almost scowled. "No," he replied sullenly, he himself "was not permitted" to know the prisoner's name. His crime? He did not know. When was he to be tried? To-morrow. Then he rose and abruptly requested the captain to ask no more questions. But, he added, with a smile, he could promise him that he should at least see the captive again.

In a few minutes a boat came off, and the prisoner, closely guarded, and with his face covered with a piece of cloth, was hurried ashore.

*   *   *   *   *

Four days had passed--days of heat so intense that even the Chinese crew of the steamer lay about the decks under the awning, stripped to their waists, and fanning themselves languidly. During this time the captain and his officers, by careful inquiries, ascertained that the unfortunate prisoner was a brother of one of the Wangs, or seven "Heavenly Kings," who had led the Taeping forces, and that for a long time past the Viceroy had made most strenuous efforts to effect his capture, being particularly exasperated with him, not only for his courage in the field, and the influence he had wielded over the unfortunate Taepings, who were wiped out by Gordon and the Ever-Victorious Army, but also because he refused to accept Li Hung Chang's sworn word to spare his life if he surrendered; for well he knew that a death by torture awaited him. Gordon himself, it was said, revolver in hand, and with tears of rage streaming down his face, had sought to find and shoot the Viceroy for the cruel murder of other leaders who had surrendered to him under the solemn promise of their lives being spared.

Late in the afternoon, a messenger came on board with a note to the captain. It was from the mandarin Kwang, and contained but a line. "Follow the bearer, who will guide you to the prisoner."

An hour later Carpenter was conducted through a narrow door which was set in a very high wall of great thickness. He found himself in a garden of the greatest beauty, and magnificent proportions. Temples and other buildings of the most elaborate and artistic design and construction showed here and there amid a profusion of gloriously-foliaged trees and flowering shrubs. No sound broke the silence except the twittering of birds; and not a single person was visible.

The guide, who had not yet uttered a single word, now turned and motioned Carpenter to follow him along a winding path, paved with white marble slabs, and bordered with gaily-hued flowers. Suddenly they emerged upon a lovely sward of the brightest green, in the centre of which a fountain played, sending its fine feathery spray high in air.

On one side of the fountain were a number of "braves" who stood in a close circle, and, as Carpenter approached, two of them silently stepped out of the cordon, brought their rifles to the salute, and the guide whispered to him to enter.

Within the circle was Kwang, who was seated in his chair of office. He rose and greeted the captain politely.

"I promised you that you should again see the criminal in whom you and your officers took such a deep and benevolent interest. I now fulfil that promise--and leave you." And, with a malevolent smile, he bowed and disappeared.

The guide touched Carpenter's arm.

"Look," he said in a whisper.

*   *   *   *   *

Within a few inches of a wavering line of spray from the fountain, purposely diverted so as to fall upon the grass, lay what appeared at first sight to be a round bundle tied up in a buffalo hide. A black swarm of flies buzzed and buzzed over and around it.

"Draw near and look," said the harsh voice of the officer who commanded the grim, silent guard, as he stepped up to the strange-looking bundle, and waved his fan quickly to and fro over a protuberance in the centre.

A black cloud of flies arose, and revealed a sight that will haunt Carpenter to his dying day--the purpled, distorted face of a living man. The eyelids had been cut off, and only two dreadful, bloodied, glaring things of horror appealed mutely to God. The victim's knees had been drawn up to his chin, and only his head was visible; for the fresh buffalo hide in which his body had been sewn, fitted tightly around his neck.

Shuddering with horror, and yet fascinated with the dreadful spectacle, Carpenter asked the officer how long the prisoner had been tortured.

"Four days," was the reply.

For the buffalo, the hide of which was to be the prisoner's death-wrap, was in readiness the moment the steamer arrived, and ten minutes after the signal was hoisted, the creature was killed, the hide stripped off, and the prisoner sewn up in it, only his head being left free.

Then he was carried to a heated room, so that the hide should contract quickly. From there he was taken to the fountain, where his eyelids were cut off, and then he was laid upon the ground, his mouth just within a few inches of a spray from the fountain.

And the Viceroy came, saw, approved, and smiled, and assigned to Kwang the honoured post of watching his hated enemy die under slow and agonising torture. To attract the flies, honeyed water was applied to the prisoner's shaven head and face. And the guards, now and then as his thirst increased, offered him brine to drink.

"He is still alive," the brutal-faced Tartar officer said genially, as he touched one of the dreadful eyeballs, and the poor, tortured creature's lips moved slightly.

Sick at heart and almost overcome with horror, Captain Carpenter, with quickened footsteps, passed through the cordon of guards, and followed his guide from the dreadful spot.

In a few minutes he was without the wall, and a sigh of relief broke from him as he set out towards the river.

A CRUISE IN THE SOUTH SEAS
(HINTS TO INTENDING TRAVELLERS)

The traveller who makes a hurried trip in an excursion steamer through the Cook, Society, Samoan, or Tongan Islands has but little opportunity of seeing anything of the social life of the natives, or getting either fishing or shooting; for it is but rarely that the vessel remains for more than forty-eight hours at any of the ports visited. Personally, if I wanted to have an enjoyable cruise among the various island groups in the South Pacific I should avoid the "excursion" steamer as I would the plague. In the first place, one sees next to nothing for his passage money if he fatuously takes a ticket in either Sydney or New Zealand for "a round trip to Tonga, Samoa, Tahiti, and back." Certainly, he will enjoy the sea voyage, for in the Australasian winter months the weather in the South Seas is never very hot, and cloudless skies and a smooth sea may almost be relied upon from April until the end of July. At such places as Nukualofa, the little capital of the Tonga Islands, an excursion steamer will remain for perhaps forty hours; at Apia, in Samoa, forty-eight hours; and at Papeite, the capital of the French island of Tahiti, forty-eight hours. At the two latter places the traveller will be charmed by the lovely scenery, and disgusted by the squalid appearance of the natives; for within the last ten years great changes have occurred, and the native communities inhabiting the island ports, such as Apia and Papeite, have degenerated into the veriest loafers, spongers, and thieves. The appearance of a strange European in any of the environs of Apia is the signal for an onslaught of beggars of all ages and both sexes, who will pester his life out for tobacco; if he says he does not smoke, they say a sixpence will do as well. If he refuses he is pretty sure to be insulted by some half-naked ruffian, and will be glad to get back to the ship or to the refuge of an hotel. And yet, away from the contaminating influences of the town the white stranger will meet with politeness and respect wherever he goes--particularly if he is an Englishman--and will at once note the pleasing difference in the manners of the natives. Yet it must now be remembered that Samoa--with the exception of the beautiful island of Tutuila--is German territory, and German officials are none too effusive to Englishmen or Americans--in Samoa.

But if any one wants to spend an enjoyable time in the South Seas let him avoid the "excursion ship" and go there in a trading steamer. There are several of these now sailing out of Australasian ports, and there is a choice of groups to visit. If a four months' voyage is not too long, a passage may be obtained in a small, but fairly fast and comfortable boat of 600 tons sailing from Sydney, which visits over forty islands in her cruise from Niue or Savage Island, ten days' steam from Sydney, to Jaluit in the Marshall Islands. But this particular cruise I would not recommend to any one in search of a variety of beautiful scenery, for nearly all of the islands visited are of the one type--low-lying sandy atolls, densely verdured with coco-palms, and very monotonous from their sameness of appearance. Their inhabitants, however, are widely different in manners, customs, and general mode of life. To the ethnologist such a cruise among the Ellice, Gilbert, and Marshall Islands would no doubt be full of interest; but to the traveller in search of either beautiful scenery or sport (except fishing) they would be disappointing.

Let us suppose that the intending traveller desires to make a stay of some two or three months in the Samoan Group. He can reach there easily enough from Sydney or Auckland by steamer once a month, either by one of the Union Steamship Company's regular traders or by one of the San Francisco mail boats. From Sydney the voyage occupies eight days, from Auckland five. The outfit required for a three or four months' stay is not a large one--light clothing can be bought almost as cheaply in Samoa as in Sydney, a couple of guns with plenty of ammunition (for cartridges are shockingly dear in the Islands), a large and varied assortment of deep-sea tackle, a rod for fresh-water or reef fishing, and a good waterproof and rugs for camping out, as the early mornings are sometimes very chilly. And there is one other thing that is worth while taking, even though it may cost from L30 to L50 or so in Sydney--a good secondhand boat, with two suits of sails. Thus provided the sportsman can sail all along the coasts of Savaii and Upolu, and be practically independent of the local storekeepers. To hire a boat is very expensive, and to travel in native craft is horribly uncomfortable, and risky as well. And such a boat can always be sold again for at least its cost.

A stay of two or three days, or at most a week, in Apia is quite long enough, and the stranger will get all the information he requires about the outlying districts from the Consuls or any of the old white residents. Such provisions as are needed--tea, sugar, flour, biscuits, tinned or other meats, &c.--can be had at fairly cheap rates; but a large stock should be taken, for, besides the keep of the native crew of, say, four men, it must always be borne in mind that a white visitor is expected to return the hospitality he receives from the native chiefs by making a present, and the Samoans are particularly susceptible to the charms of tinned meats, sardines, salmon, and *falaoa* (bread or biscuit). That such a return should be made is only just and natural, though I am sorry to say that very often it is not. Then, again, it is very easy to stow away in the trade box in the boat eight or ten pieces of good print, cut off in pieces of six fathoms (which is enough to make a woman's gown), about 30 lbs. of twist negrohead tobacco (twenty to thirty sticks to the pound), half a gross of lucifer matches, and such things as cotton, scissors, combs, &c., and powder, caps, and a bag of No. 3 shot for pigeon shooting. Now, this seems a lot of articles for a man to take on a short Samoan *malaga* (journey), but it is not, and for the L50 which it may cost for such an outfit (exclusive of the boat and crew's wages) the traveller will see more of the people and their mode of life, be more hospitably received, and spend a pleasanter time than if he were cruising about in a 1,000-ton yacht. The wages or boatmen and native sailors in Samoa are usually $15.00 per month, but many will gladly go on a *malaga* (the general acceptance of the word is a pleasure trip) for much less, for there is but little work, and much eating and drinking. But, as sailors, the Samoans are a wretched lot, and the local living Savage Islanders, as the natives of Niue Island are called, are far better, especially if there is any wind or a beat to windward in a heavy sea. These Savage Island "boys" can always be obtained in Apia. They are good seamen and very willing to work; but they have to be fed entirely by their white employer, for the Samoans seldom make a present of food to a crew of Niue boys, for whom they profess a contempt and designate *au puaa--i.e.*, pigs.

The Samoan Group consists of five islands, trending from west by north to east by south. The two largest are Upolu and Savaii. Tutuila, and the Manua Group of three islands are too far to the windward to attempt in a small boat against the south-east trades. And it would take quite three months to visit the principal villages on the two large islands, staying a few days at each place.

The best plan is to make to windward along the coast of Upolu after leaving Apia. A large boat cannot be taken all the way inside the reef, owing to the many coral patches which, at low tide, render this course impracticable. The first place of any importance is Saluafata, fifteen miles from Apia (I must mention that Apia is in the centre of Upolu, and on the north side), then Falifa|, an exquisitely pretty place, and then Fa|goloa Bay and village, eight miles further on. This is the deepest indentation in Samoa, except the famous Pa|go Pa|go Harbour on Tutuila, and the scenery is very beautiful. After leaving Fa|goloa, the open sea has to be taken, for there is now no barrier reef for ten miles, where it begins at Samusu village, to the towns of Aleipata and Lepa|, two of the best in the group, and inhabited by cleanly and hospitable people. This is the weather point of Upolu, and after leaving Lepa| the boat has a clear run of over sixty miles before the glorious trades to the lee end of the island--that is, unless a stay is made at the populous towns of Falealilli, Sa|fata, Lafa|ga, and Falelatai, on the southern coast. The scenery along this part of the island is enchanting, but sudden squalls at night-time are sometimes frequent, from December to March, and 'tis always advisable to run into a port at sunset.

Two miles off the lee end of Upolu is the low-lying island of Manono, which is, however, enclosed in the Upolu barrier reef. It is only about three miles in circumference, exceedingly fertile, and is the most important place in the group, owing to the political influence wielded by the chiefly families who have always made it their home. A mile from Manono, and in the centre of the deep strait separating Upolu from Savaii, is a curiously picturesque spot, an island named Apolima.[17] It is an extinct crater, but has a narrow passage on the north side, and is inhabited by about fifty people, who are delighted to see any *papalagi* (foreigner) who is venturesome enough to make a landing there.

Savaii is distant about ten miles from Upolu. Its coast is for the most part *itu papa*--i.e., iron bound--but there are five populous towns there--Palaulae, Salealua, Asaua, Matautu, and Safune. After making the round of Savaii, the boat has to make back to Manono, and then can proceed inside the reef all the way to Apia, making stoppages at the many minor villages which stud the shore at intervals of every few miles.

These *malaga* by boat along the coast or from one island to another are much in favour with many of the white residents of Samoa, who find their life in Apia very monotonous. European ladies frequently accompany their husbands, and sometimes quite a large party is made up. More than five-and-twenty years ago, when the writer was gaining his first experiences of Samoan life, it was his good fortune to be one of such a party, and a right merry time he had of it among the natives; for in those days, although there was party warfare occasionally, the group was free from the savage hatreds and dissensions--largely fomented by the interference and intrigues of unscrupulous traders and incapable officials--which for the past ten or twelve years have made it notorious.

In travelling in Samoa one need not always rely upon native hospitality. Though most of the white traders at the outlying villages nowadays make nothing beyond a scanty living, they are as a rule very hospitable and pleased to see and entertain white visitors as well as their poor means will allow, and in nine cases out of ten would feel hurt if they were ignored and the native teacher's house visited first; for between the average trader and the native teacher there is always a natural and yet reasonable jealousy. And here let me say a word in praise of the Samoan teacher--in Samoa. Away from his native land, in charge of a mission station in another part of Polynesia or Melanesia, he is too often pompous and overbearing alike to his flock and to the white trader. Here he is far from the control and supervision of the white missionaries, who only visit him twice in the year, and consequently he thinks himself a man of vast importance. But in Samoa his superiors are prompt to curb any inclination he may evince to ride the high horse over his flock or interfere with any matter not strictly connected with his charge. So, in Samoa, the native teacher is generally a good fellow, the soul of hospitality, and anxious to entertain any chance white visitor; and although the Samoans are not bigoted ranters like the Tongans or Fijians, and the teachers have not anything like the undue and improper influence over the people possessed by the native ministers in Tonga or Fiji, to needlessly offend one would be resented by the villagers and make the visitor's stay anything but pleasant. As for the white missionaries in Samoa, all I need say of them is that they are gentlemen, and that the words "Mission House" are synonymous in most cases with warm welcome to the traveller.

Travelling inland in Savaii or crossing Upolu from north to south, or *vice-ver-sa,* is very delightful, though one misses much of the lovely scenery that unfolds itself in a panorama-like manner when sailing along the coast. One journey that can easily be accomplished in a day is that from Apia to Safata. Carriers are easily obtainable, and some splendid pigeon shooting can be had an hour or two after leaving Apia till within a few miles of Safata. Pigeons are about the only game to be had in Samoa, though the *manutagi*, or ring-dove, is very plentiful, but one hardly likes to shoot such dear little creatures. Occasionally one may get a wild duck or two and some fearful-looking wild fowls--the progeny of the domestic fowl. Wild pigs are not now plentiful in Upolu though they are in Savaii, but they are exceedingly difficult to shoot and the country they frequent is fearfully rough. In some of the streams there are some very good fish, running up to 2 lbs. or 3 lbs. They bite eagerly at the *ula* or freshwater prawn, and are excellent eating; and yet, strange to say, very few of the white residents in the group even know of their existence. This applies also to deep-sea fishing; for although the deep water outside the reefs and the passages leading into the harbours teem with splendid fish, the residents of Apia are content to buy the wretched things brought to them by women who capture them in nets in the shallow water inside the reef. Once, during my stay on Manono, a young Manhiki half-caste and myself went out in our boat about a mile from the land, and in thirty fathoms of water caught in an hour three large-scaled fish of the groper species. These fish, though once familiar enough to the people of the island, are now never fished for, and our appearance with our prizes caused quite an excitement in the village, everyone thronging around us to look. And yet there are two or three varieties of groper--many of them weighing 50 lbs. or 60 lbs.--which can be caught anywhere on the Samoan coast; but the Samoan of the present day has sadly degenerated, and, except bonito catching, deep-sea fishing is one of the lost arts. But at almost any place in the group, except Apia, great quantities of fish are caught inside the reefs by nets, and one may always be sure of getting a splendid mullet of some sort for either breakfast or supper.

Let us suppose that a party of Europeans have arrived at a village, and are the guests of the chief and people generally. Food is at once brought to them, even before any visits of ceremony are paid, for the news of the coming of a party of travellers has doubtless been brought to the village the previous day by a messenger from the last stopping-place. The repast provided may be simple, but will be ample, baked pork most likely being the *piece de resistance,* with roast fowl, baked pigeons, breadfruit (if in season), and yams or taro, with a plentiful supply of young drinking-coconuts. (Should the host be the local teacher, some deplorable tea and a loaf of terrible bread are sure to be produced.) This preliminary meal finished, the formalities begin by a visit from the chief and his *tulafale,* or "talking-man," accompanied by the leading citizens. The talking-man then makes a speech, welcoming the guests, and is by no means sparing of "buttery" phrases which indicate the intense delight, &c., of the inhabitants of the village at having the honoured privilege of entertaining such noble and distinguished visitors, &c. A suitable reply is made by the guests (through an interpreter, if no one among them can speak Samoan), and then follows a ceremonious brewing and drinking of kava. This is a most important function in Samoa, and to the stranger unaccustomed to the manner of making the beverage, the ordeal of drinking it is an exceedingly trying one. It is prepared as follows: The dried kava root is cut up in thin slices and handed to a number of young women, who masticate it and then deposit it in a large wooden *tanoa*, or bowl. Water is then added in sufficient quantity till the *tanoa* is half-filled with a thin yellowish-green liquid, which is carefully strained by a thick "swab" of the beaten bark of the *fau*-tree. This straining operation is performed only by a very experienced lady, and is watched in respectful silence. Then the drink is handed round in a polished bowl of coconut-shell. But for a full description of all the details of a kava-drinking, let me commend my readers to the best and most charming book ever written on South Sea life, "South Sea Bubbles," by the late Earl of Pembroke and Dr. Kingsley. Nowadays, however, many Samoan households, out of deference to European tastes, have the kava root grated instead of being chewed.

The kava-drinking over, all stiffness and formality disappears for the time, and the visitors are surrounded by the villagers, eager to learn the latest news from Apia, and from the world abroad. The discussion of political matters always has a strong attraction for Samoans, who are anxious to learn the state of affairs in Europe, and their knowledge and shrewdness is surprising. Should there be any white ladies present, the brown ones make much of them. The Samoans are a fine, handsome race, and the faces and figures of many of the young women are very attractive; but the practice of cutting off their long, flowing black hair, and allowing it to grow in a short, stiff "frizz" is all too common, and detracts very much from an otherwise handsome and graceful appearance, especially when the hair is coated with lime in order to change its colour to red. Many of the men, particularly those of chiefly rank, are of magnificent stature and proportions, and their walk and carriage are in consonance.

An announcement that the visitors intend to go pigeon shooting is warmly applauded, and each white man is at once provided with a guide, for, unless he has had experience of the Samoan forest, he will return with an empty bag, as, however plentiful the birds may be, their habit of hiding in the branches of the lofty *tamanu* and *masa'oi*-trees render them difficult of detection. The natives themselves are very good shots, and very rarely fail to bring down a bird, even when nothing more than a scarlet leg or a blue-grey feather is visible. The guns they use are very common, cheap German affairs, but are specially made for Samoa, being very small bored and long in the barrel. The best time is in the early morning and towards the cool of the evening, when the birds are feeding on *masa'oi* and other berries; during the heat of the day they seldom leave their perches, though their deep crooning note may be heard everywhere. In the mountainous interiors of Upolu and Savaii there is but little undergrowth; the ground is carpeted with a thick layer of leaves, dry on the top, but rain and dew-soaked beneath, and simply to breathe the sweet, cool mountain air is delightful. At certain times of the year the birds are very fat, and I have very often seen them literally burst when striking the ground after being shot in high trees. Their flavour is delicious, especially if they are hung for a day. I may here remark that, in New Britain, precisely the same species of pigeon is very often quite uneatable through feeding upon Chili berries, which in that island grow in profusion. In shooting in a Samoan forest one has nothing to fear from venomous reptiles, for, although there are two or three kinds of snakes, they are rarely ever seen and quite harmless. Scorpions and centipedes--the latter often six inches in length--there are in plenty, but these detestable vermin are more common in European habitations than in the bush. At the same time, mosquitoes are a terrible annoyance anywhere in the vicinity of water, and delight in attacking the tender skin of the stranger. Then, again, beware of scratching any exposed part of the skin, for, unless it is quickly covered by plaister or otherwise attended to, an irritating sore, which may take months to heal, will often result.

There are, during the visit of a travelling party to a Samoan town, no fixed times for meals. You are expected to eat much and often. During the day there will be continuous arrivals of people bringing baskets of provisions as presents, which are formally presented--with a speech. The speech has to be responded to, and the bringers of the presents treated politely, as long as they remain, and they remain until their curiosity--and avarice--is satisfied. A return present must be sent on the following day; for although Samoans designate every present of food or anything else made to a party of visitors as an "alofa"--*i.e.,* a gift of love--this is but a hollow conventionalism, it being the time-honoured custom of the country to always give a *quid pro quo* for whatever has been received. Yet it must not be imagined that they are a selfish people; if the recipients of an "alofa" of food are too poor to respond otherwise than by a profusion of thanks, the donors of the "alofa" are satisfied--it would be a disgrace for their village to be spoken of as having treated guests meanly.

After evening service--conducted on week-days in each house by the head of the family--another meal is served. Then either lamps or a fire of coconut-shells is lit, and there is a great making of *sului*, or cigarettes of strong tobacco rolled in dry banana leaf, and there is much merry jostling and shoving among the young lads and girls for a seat on the matted floor, to hear the white people talk. A dance is sure to be suggested, and presently the *fale po-ula,* or dance-house, is lit up in preparation, as the dancers, male and female, hurry away to adorn themselves. Much has been said about the impropriety of Samoa dancing by travellers who have only witnessed the degrading and indecent exhibitions, given on a large scale by the loafing class of natives who inhabit Apia and its immediate vicinity. The natives are an adaptive race, and suit their manners to their company, and there are always numbers of sponging men and *paumotu* (beach-women) ready to pander to the tastes of low whites who are willing to witness a lewd dance. But in most villages, situated away from the contaminating influences of the principal port, a native *siva*, or dance, is well worth witnessing, and the accompanying singing is very melodious. It is, however, true, that on important occasions, such as the marriage of a great chief, &c., that the dancing, decorous enough in the earlier stages of the evening, degenerates under the influence of excitement into an exhibition that provokes sorrow and disgust. And yet, curiously enough, the dancers at these times are not low class, common people, but young men and women of high lineage, who, led by the *taupo*, or maid of the village, cast aside all restraint and modesty. In many of the dances the costumes are exceedingly pretty, the men wearing aprons made of the yellow and scarlet leaves of the *ti* or dracoena plant, with head-dresses formed of pieces of iridescent pearl-shell, intermixed with silver coins and scarlet and amber beads, and the hair of both sexes is profusely adorned with the scarlet flowers of the hibiscus, while from their necks depend large strings of *sea-sea, masa'oi,* and other brightly-coloured and sweet-smelling berries. Of late years the Tahitian fashion of wearing thick wreaths of orange or lemon blossoms has come into vogue.

Before concluding these remarks upon Samoa, I must mention that the climate is very healthy for the greater part of the year; but in the rainy season, December to March, the heat is intense, and sickness is often prevalent, especially in Apia. Still fever, such as is met with in the New Hebrides and the Solomon Group, "the grave of the white man in the South Seas," is unknown, and one may sleep in the open air with impunity. Before setting out from Apia the services of a competent interpreter should be secured--a man who thoroughly understands the Samoan *customs* as well as the language. Plenty of reliable half-castes can always be found, any one of whom would be glad to engage for a very moderate payment. Too often the pleasures of such a trip as I have described have been marred by the interpreter's lack of tact and knowledge of the idiosyncrasies of the inhabitants of the various districts and villages. The mere fact of a man being able to speak the language fairly well is not the all in all; for the Samoans are a highly sensitive people, and the omission by the interpreter of a chief's titles, &c., when the guests are responding through him to an address of welcome, would be considered "shockingly bad form."

But the reader must not imagine that the Samoan Group is the only one in the South Pacific where an enjoyable holiday may be spent. The French possession of the Society Islands, of which the pretty town Papeite, in the noble island of Tahiti, is the capital, rivals, if not exceeds, Samoa in the magnificence of its scenery, and the natives are a highly intelligent race of Malayo-Polynesians who, despite their being citizens of the French Republic, never forget that they were redeemed from savagery by Englishmen, and a *taata Peretane* (Englishman) is an ever-welcome guest to them. The facilities for visiting the different islands of the Society Group are very good, for there is quite a fleet of native and European-owned vessels constantly cruising throughout the archipelago. To cross the island of Tahiti from its south-east to its north-west point is one of the most delightful trips imaginable. Then again, the Hervey or Cook's Group, which consist of the fertile islands of Mangaia, Rarotonga, Atui, Aitutaki, and Mauki, are well worth visiting. The people speak a language similar to that of Tahiti, and they are a fine, hospitable race, albeit a little over-civilised. Both of these groups can be reached from Auckland by sailing vessels, but not direct from Sydney. As for the lonely islands of the North Pacific, they are too far afield for any one to visit but the trader or the traveller to whom time is nothing.

NOTES

1: Literally, "clear crony."

2: Port.

3: Happiness.

4: A libertine, profligate.

5: My love to you, Pakia; are you well?

6: White foreigners.

7: Frank.

8: Small-pox.

9: An accordion.

10: Idler, gad about--a Samoan expression.

11: German.

12: The Tokelau and Ellice Islanders are much amused at the white man's method of hauling in a heavy fish hand *over* hand. This to them is "*faka fafine*"--i.e., like a woman.

13: Cayse.

14: NOTE BY THE PUBLISHER.--This incident is related by the author in "By Reef and Palm" under the title of "The Rangers of the Tia Kau."

15: PUBLISHER'S NOTE.--This Alan Strickland is the "Allan" who has so frequently figured in the author's other tales of South Sea life, notably in the works entitled "By Reef and Palm" and "The Ebbing of the Tide."

16: Councillors.

17: *Apo! lima*! "Be quick with your hand!" The passage is narrow and dangerous, even for canoes, and the steersman, as he watches the rolling surf, calls out *Apo, lau lima*! to his crew--an expression synonymous to our nautical, "Pull like the devil!"

The Codes Of Hammurabi And Moses
W. W. Davies

QTY

The discovery of the Hammurabi Code is one of the greatest achievements of archaeology, and is of paramount interest, not only to the student of the Bible, but also to all those interested in ancient history...

Religion   **ISBN:** *1-59462-338-4*   **Pages:132**
MSRP $12.95

The Theory of Moral Sentiments
Adam Smith

QTY

This work from 1749. contains original theories of conscience amd moral judgment and it is the foundation for systemof morals.

Philosophy   ISBN: *1-59462-777-0*   **Pages:536**
MSRP $19.95

Jessica's First Prayer
Hesba Stretton

QTY

In a screened and secluded corner of one of the many railway-bridges which span the streets of London there could be seen a few years ago, from five o'clock every morning until half past eight, a tidily set-out coffee-stall, consisting of a trestle and board, upon which stood two large tin cans, with a small fire of charcoal burning under each so as to keep the coffee boiling during the early hours of the morning when the work-people were thronging into the city on their way to their daily toil...

Pages:84

Childrens   ISBN: *1-59462-373-2*   *MSRP $9.95*

My Life and Work
Henry Ford

QTY

Henry Ford revolutionized the world with his implementation of mass production for the Model T automobile. Gain valuable business insight into his life and work with his own auto-biography... "We have only started on our development of our country we have not as yet, with all our talk of wonderful progress, done more than scratch the surface. The progress has been wonderful enough but..."

Pages:300

Biographies/   **ISBN:** *1-59462-198-5*   *MSRP $21.95*

The Art of Cross-Examination
Francis Wellman

QTY

I presume it is the experience of every author, after his first book is published upon an important subject, to be almost overwhelmed with a wealth of ideas and illustrations which could readily have been included in his book, and which to his own mind, at least, seem to make a second edition inevitable. Such certainly was the case with me; and when the first edition had reached its sixth impression in five months, I rejoiced to learn that it seemed to my publishers that the book had met with a sufficiently favorable reception to justify a second and considerably enlarged edition. ..

Pages:412

Reference   ISBN: *1-59462-647-2*   *MSRP $19.95*

On the Duty of Civil Disobedience
Henry David Thoreau

QTY

Thoreau wrote his famous essay, On the Duty of Civil Disobedience, as a protest against an unjust but popular war and the immoral but popular institution of slave-owning. He did more than write—he declined to pay his taxes, and was hauled off to gaol in consequence. Who can say how much this refusal of his hastened the end of the war and of slavery ?

Law   ISBN: *1-59462-747-9*   **Pages:48**

MSRP $7.45

Dream Psychology Psychoanalysis for Beginners
Sigmund Freud

QTY

Sigmund Freud, born Sigismund Schlomo Freud (May 6, 1856 - September 23, 1939), was a Jewish-Austrian neurologist and psychiatrist who co-founded the psychoanalytic school of psychology. Freud is best known for his theories of the unconscious mind, especially involving the mechanism of repression; his redefinition of sexual desire as mobile and directed towards a wide variety of objects; and his therapeutic techniques, especially his understanding of transference in the therapeutic relationship and the presumed value of dreams as sources of insight into unconscious desires.

Pages:196

Psychology   ISBN: *1-59462-905-6*   *MSRP $15.45*

The Miracle of Right Thought
Orison Swett Marden

QTY

Believe with all of your heart that you will do what you were made to do. When the mind has once formed the habit of holding cheerful, happy, prosperous pictures, it will not be easy to form the opposite habit. It does not matter how improbable or how far away this realization may see, or how dark the prospects may be, if we visualize them as best we can, as vividly as possible, hold tenaciously to them and vigorously struggle to attain them, they will gradually become actualized, realized in the life. But a desire, a longing without endeavor, a yearning abandoned or held indifferently will vanish without realization.

Pages:360

Self Help   ISBN: *1-59462-644-8*   *MSRP $25.45*

QTY

The Rosicrucian Cosmo-Conception Mystic Christianity by *Max Heindel*   ISBN: *1-59462-188-8*   **$38.95**
The Rosicrucian Cosmo-conception is not dogmatic, neither does it appeal to any other authority than the reason of the student. It is: not controversial, but is: sent forth in the, hope that it may help to clear...   New Age/Religion Pages 646

Abandonment To Divine Providence by *Jean-Pierre de Caussade*   ISBN: *1-59462-228-0*   **$25.95**
"The Rev. Jean Pierre de Caussade was one of the most remarkable spiritual writers of the Society of Jesus in France in the 18th Century. His death took place at Toulouse in 1751. His works have gone through many editions and have been republished...   Inspirational/Religion Pages 400

Mental Chemistry by *Charles Haanel*   ISBN: *1-59462-192-6*   **$23.95**
Mental Chemistry allows the change of material conditions by combining and appropriately utilizing the power of the mind. Much like applied chemistry creates something new and unique out of careful combinations of chemicals the mastery of mental chemistry...   New Age Pages 354

The Letters of Robert Browning and Elizabeth Barret Barrett 1845-1846 vol II   ISBN: *1-59462-193-4*   **$35.95**
by *Robert Browning* and *Elizabeth Barrett*   Biographies Pages 596

Gleanings In Genesis (volume I) by *Arthur W. Pink*   ISBN: *1-59462-130-6*   **$27.45**
Appropriately has Genesis been termed "the seed plot of the Bible" for in it we have, in germ form, almost all of the great doctrines which are afterwards fully developed in the books of Scripture which follow...   Religion/Inspirational Pages 420

The Master Key by *L. W. de Laurence*   ISBN: *1-59462-001-6*   **$30.95**
In no branch of human knowledge has there been a more lively increase of the spirit of research during the past few years than in the study of Psychology, Concentration and Mental Discipline. The requests for authentic lessons in Thought Control, Mental Discipline and...   New Age/Business Pages 422

The Lesser Key Of Solomon Goetia by *L. W. de Laurence*   ISBN: *1-59462-092-X*   **$9.95**
This translation of the first book of the "Lernegton" which is now for the first time made accessible to students of Talismanic Magic was done, after careful collation and edition, from numerous Ancient Manuscripts in Hebrew, Latin, and French...   New Age/Occult Pages 92

Rubaiyat Of Omar Khayyam by *Edward Fitzgerald*   ISBN: *1-59462-332-5*   **$13.95**
Edward Fitzgerald, whom the world has already learned, in spite of his own efforts to remain within the shadow of anonymity, to look upon as one of the rarest poets of the century, was born at Bredfield, in Suffolk, on the 31st of March, 1809. He was the third son of John Purcell...   Music Pages 172

Ancient Law by *Henry Maine*   ISBN: *1-59462-128-4*   **$29.95**
The chief object of the following pages is to indicate some of the earliest ideas of mankind, as they are reflected in Ancient Law, and to point out the relation of those ideas to modern thought.   Religion/History Pages 452

Far-Away Stories by *William J. Locke*   ISBN: *1-59462-129-2*   **$19.45**
"Good wine needs no bush, but a collection of mixed vintages does. And this book is just such a collection. Some of the stories I do not want to remain buried for ever in the museum files of dead magazine-numbers an author's not unpardonable vanity..."   Fiction Pages 272

Life of David Crockett by *David Crockett*   ISBN: *1-59462-250-7*   **$27.45**
"Colonel David Crockett was one of the most remarkable men of the times in which he lived. Born in humble life, but gifted with a strong will, an indomitable courage, and unremitting perseverance...   Biographies/New Age Pages 424

Lip-Reading by *Edward Nitchie*   ISBN: *1-59462-206-X*   **$25.95**
Edward B. Nitchie, founder of the New York School for the Hard of Hearing, now the Nitchie School of Lip-Reading, Inc, wrote "LIP-READING Principles and Practice". The development and perfecting of this meritorious work on lip-reading was an undertaking...   How-to Pages 400

A Handbook of Suggestive Therapeutics, Applied Hypnotism, Psychic Science   ISBN: *1-59462-214-0*   **$24.95**
by *Henry Munro*   Health/New Age/Health/Self-help Pages 376

A Doll's House: and Two Other Plays by *Henrik Ibsen*   ISBN: *1-59462-112-8*   **$19.95**
Henrik Ibsen created this classic when in revolutionary 1848 Rome. Introducing some striking concepts in playwriting for the realist genre, this play has been studied the world over.   Fiction/Classics/Plays 308

The Light of Asia by *sir Edwin Arnold*   ISBN: *1-59462-204-3*   **$13.95**
In this poetic masterpiece, Edwin Arnold describes the life and teachings of Buddha. The man who was to become known as Buddha to the world was born as Prince Gautama of India but he rejected the worldly riches and abandoned the reigns of power when...   Religion/History/Biographies Pages 170

The Complete Works of Guy de Maupassant by *Guy de Maupassant*   ISBN: *1-59462-157-8*   **$16.95**
"For days and days, nights and nights, I had dreamed of that first kiss which was to consecrate our engagement, and I knew not on what spot I should put my lips..."   Fiction/Classics Pages 240

The Art of Cross-Examination by *Francis L. Wellman*   ISBN: *1-59462-309-0*   **$26.95**
Written by a renowned trial lawyer, Wellman imparts his experience and uses case studies to explain how to use psychology to extract desired information through questioning.   How-to/Science/Reference Pages 408

Answered or Unanswered? by *Louisa Vaughan*   ISBN: *1-59462-248-5*   **$10.95**
Miracles of Faith in China   Religion Pages 112

The Edinburgh Lectures on Mental Science (1909) by *Thomas*   ISBN: *1-59462-008-3*   **$11.95**
This book contains the substance of a course of lectures recently given by the writer in the Queen Street Hall, Edinburgh. Its purpose is to indicate the Natural Principles governing the relation between Mental Action and Material Conditions...   New Age/Psychology Pages 148

Ayesha by *H. Rider Haggard*   ISBN: *1-59462-301-5*   **$24.95**
Verily and indeed it is the unexpected that happens! Probably if there was one person upon the earth from whom the Editor of this, and of a certain previous history, did not expect to hear again...   Classics Pages 380

Ayala's Angel by *Anthony Trollope*   ISBN: *1-59462-352-X*   **$29.95**
The two girls were both pretty, but Lucy who was twenty-one who supposed to be simple and comparatively unattractive, whereas Ayala was credited, as her Bombwhat romantic name might show, with poetic charm and a taste for romance. Ayala when her father died was nineteen...   Fiction Pages 484

The American Commonwealth by *James Bryce*   ISBN: *1-59462-286-8*   **$34.45**
An interpretation of American democratic political theory. It examines political mechanics and society from the perspective of Scotsman James Bryce   Politics Pages 572

Stories of the Pilgrims by *Margaret P. Pumphrey*   ISBN: *1-59462-116-0*   **$17.95**
This book explores pilgrims religious oppression in England as well as their escape to Holland and eventual crossing to America on the Mayflower, and their early days in New England...   History Pages 268

QTY

The Fasting Cure *by Sinclair Upton*
In the Cosmopolitan Magazine for May, 1910, and in the Contemporary Review (London) for April, 1910, I published an article dealing with my experiences in fasting. I have written a great many magazine articles, but never one which attracted so much attention... New Age/Self Help/Health Pages 164

ISBN: *1-59462-222-1* **$13.95**

Hebrew Astrology *by Sepharial*
In these days of advanced thinking it is a matter of common observation that we have left many of the old landmarks behind and that we are now pressing forward to greater heights and to a wider horizon than that which represented the mind-content of our progenitors... Astrology Pages 144

ISBN: *1-59462-308-2* **$13.45**

Thought Vibration or The Law of Attraction in the Thought World
by William Walker Atkinson
Psychology/Religion Pages 144

ISBN: *1-59462-127-6* **$12.95**

Optimism *by Helen Keller*
Helen Keller was blind, deaf, and mute since 19 months old, yet famously learned how to overcome these handicaps, communicate with the world, and spread her lectures promoting optimism. An inspiring read for everyone... Biographies/Inspirational Pages 84

ISBN: *1-59462-108-X* **$15.95**

Sara Crewe *by Frances Burnett*
In the first place, Miss Minchin lived in London. Her home was a large, dull, tall one, in a large, dull square, where all the houses were alike, and all the sparrows were alike, and where all the door-knockers made the same heavy sound... Childrens/Classic Pages 88

ISBN: *1-59462-360-0* **$9.45**

The Autobiography of Benjamin Franklin *by Benjamin Franklin*
The Autobiography of Benjamin Franklin has probably been more extensively read than any other American historical work, and no other book of its kind has had such ups and downs of fortune. Franklin lived for many years in England, where he was agent... Biographies/History Pages 332

ISBN: *1-59462-135-7* **$24.95**

Name	
Email	
Telephone	
Address	
City, State ZIP	

☐ **Credit Card**   ☐ **Check / Money Order**

Credit Card Number	
Expiration Date	
Signature	

Please Mail to: Book Jungle
PO Box 2226
Champaign, IL 61825
or Fax to: 630-214-0564

www.ingramcontent.com/pod-product-compliance
Lightning Source LLC
Chambersburg PA
CBHW080908020726
47502CB00008B/2393